BAMBI

Felix Salten

Translated by Hannah Correll

CLYDESDALE

First published in 1923 by Ullstein Verlag

First Clydesdale Press Edition 2019

Translation © 2019 by Clydesdale Press

Clydesdale books may be purchased in bulk at special discounts for sales promotion, corporate gifts, fund-raising, or educational purposes. Special editions can also be created to specifications. For details, contact the Special Sales Department, Skyhorse Publishing, 307 West 36th Street, 11th Floor, New York, NY 10018 or info@skyhorsepublishing.com.

Clydesdale Press™ is a pending trademark of Skyhorse Publishing, Inc.®, a Delaware corporation.

Visit our website at www.skyhorsepublishing.com.

10 9 8 7 6 5 4 3 2 1

Library of Congress Cataloging-in-Publication Data is available on file.

Series design by Brian Peterson
Cover artwork credit: iStockphoto

Print ISBN: 978-1-949846-05-8
eISBN: 978-1-949846-06-5

Printed in the United States of America

CHAPTER I

He came into the world in the middle of a thicket—in a hidden clearing in the woods—the kind that seems to be open in all directions, but still is covered by a canopy. It was a small space, hardly enough room for him and his mother.

There he stood, swaying timidly on his thin legs, looking drowsily around him through cloudy eyes, which saw nothing, letting his head droop, trembling mightily, and he was still quite numb.

"What a beautiful child!" called out a magpie.

She had flown by, lured in by the startling moans from the mother's labor. Now the magpie sat on a branch nearby. "What a beautiful child!" she called out. She received no answer and continued on eagerly. "How amazing that it can even stand and walk! How interesting! I have never before, in all my life, seen such a thing. Admittedly, I am still young, just out of the nest for a year, as you may know. But how wonderful! Such a sweet child . . . born in this moment and can already stand on its own legs. I find it so noble. I find everything about you deer is so noble. Can he walk already . . . ?"

"Of course," replied the mother quietly. "But you must excuse me if I am not able to chat. I have so much to do right now . . . besides I still feel a bit weary."

"Please do not let me disturb you," said the magpie, "I do not have much time myself. But it is not every day that you get to see such a sight. I say, how cumbersome and difficult it is in these moments. The children cannot move when they first hatch from the egg, they lay there so helplessly in the nest and you must care for them. Care for them. I tell you, I can make no sense of it. Oh, what tireless work it is to feed them, how carefully I must watch over them. I say, think how hard it is to gather food for the children and at the same time look after them so that no danger should come to them; they cannot help themselves when they are alone. Do you not agree? And how long must we wait until they can move on their own, how long does it take them to get their feathers and look proper!"

"I beg your pardon," replied the mother, "I wasn't listening to you."

The magpie flew away. "What a strange person," she thought to herself, "noble, but strange!"

The mother hardly realized it. She continued to eagerly wash the newborn. She washed it with her tongue; it was grooming, warming massage, and caress all at once.

The little one wobbled a bit. He folded together from the all the gentle, jostling licks and nudging and became still. His small red back, which was still a bit tousled, had fine white dots, and his drowsy infant-like face had the expression of deep sleep.

Hazelnut, dogwood, blackthorn, and young elderberry grew all around. Tall maple, beech, and oak trees built a green roof over the thicket and the firm, dark brown ground sprouted forth fern fronds, sweet pea, and sage. Leaves of violets which had already bloomed, and strawberries which were just beginning to bloom, nestled close to the ground. The light of the early morning sun permeated the thick foliage like a golden web. A mix of voices rang throughout the entire forest and infused it with joyous excitement. The oriole whooped relentlessly, the pigeons cooed ceaselessly, the blackbirds whistled, the finches flapped, the titmice chirped; this gentle chorus of music was disturbed only by the quarrelsome cries of the jays, the blaring laughter of the magpies, and the metallic bursting of the pheasants' calls, like bells. Sometimes the shrill, short laughter of a woodpecker rose above all the other voices. Above the treetops, the falcon's cry, bright and urgent, could be heard, and the crows let out a constant choir of their cries.

The little one understood not a single one of the many songs and shrieks, nor a word of the conversations. He listened not at all. He did not perceive the scents which the forest breathed. He only heard the soft rustling which ran along his back as he was washed, warmed, and kissed, and he smelled nothing but the close scent of his mother. He snuggled up to this comforting presence and searched hungrily to find therein the source of his food.

While he drank, the mother continued to caress the little one. "Bambi," she whispered.

In this moment, she lifted her head; her ears perked up and listened to the wind.

Then she kissed her child again, calm and happy. "Bambi," she repeated, "my little Bambi."

CHAPTER 2

Now in the early summer, the trees stood still under the blue sky, held their arms outstretched, and received the energy that beamed down from the sun. The blossoms on the hedges and bushes in the thicket opened—white, red, and yellow stars. Some even began to bear young fruit—innumerable small, balled up fists, perched on the fine tips of branches, delicate and firm and determined. These colorful stars came up from the ground amongst a multitude of flowers, so that the woodland ground seemed to sparkle in the dawn. It smelled of fresh leaves, flowers, damp earth, and green wood. When morning broke and when the sun set, the entire forest sounded a thousand voices, and from morning until evening the bees sang, the wasps hummed, and the bumblebees bumbled through the fragrant silence.

So were the first days of Bambi's childhood.

He walked behind his mother along a narrow path that ran through the bushes. How calm it was to wander this path! The thick foliage gently caressed his sides and bent ever so slightly to the side. The path seemed to be blocked and barricaded tenfold in each direction. However, they were able to move through it with the most comfort. Such paths were everywhere; they ran here and there throughout the entire forest. His mother knew them all and when Bambi stood before dense undergrowth like an impassable green wall, his mother always found a spot where the path led on, without stopping and searching.

Bambi asked many questions. He loved to ask his mother questions. It was the most wonderful thing for him, asking questions and listening to his mother's reply. Bambi was hardly astonished that he constantly and effortlessly thought of question after question. He found it to be quite natural; it delighted him so. It delighted him also to wait, curiously, until the answer came. Sometimes he admittedly did not understand her, but even that was lovely, as he could always keep asking questions if he wanted. Sometimes he did not continue asking, and that was also lovely, because he then busied himself imagining what he had not understood in his own way. Sometimes he felt quite sure that his mother did not offer him a full answer and kept some of her knowledge to herself. And even this was even more lovely, for it left him with an even more special curiosity—a clue that made him search secretly, an expectation that made him anxiously cheerful, so much so that he fell silent.

Now he asked, "Who does this path belong to, mother?"
His mother answered, "Us."
Bambi continued, "You and I?"
"Yes."
"Both of us?"
"Yes."
"Just us?"
"No," said his mother, "we deer . . ."
"What is deer?" asked Bambi and laughed.

His mother looked at him and laughed, too. "You are a deer, and I am a deer. That is what deer is. Do you understand?"

Bambi sprung into the air with laughter. "Yes, I understood that! I am a little deer and you are a big deer. Right?"

His mother nodded to him. "There you have it."

Bambi became serious once more, "Are there other deer besides you and me?"

"Of course," said his mother. "Many."

"Where are they?" called Bambi.

"Here, everywhere."

"But . . . I don't see them."

"You will see them soon."

"When?" Bambi stood still, frozen with curiosity.

"Soon." His mother continued on calmly.

Bambi followed her. He was silent, because he was pondering what that could mean, "soon". He decided that "soon" was probably not the same as "right away" but close. But he could not decide on it—when does "soon" stop being "soon" and become "right away"? Suddenly, he asked, "Who made this path?"

"We did," replied his mother.

Bambi looked astounded. "We? You and I?"

His mother said, "Well, we did . . . we deer."

Bambi asked, "Who?"

"All of us," his mother replied quickly.

She continued onwards. Bambi was amused and wanted to bound off the path here and there, but he refrained and stayed with his mother. There was a loud rustling ahead of them on the forest floor. Something was moving about, hidden by the fern fronds and leaves. A thin voice cried out pitifully, then it was silent. Then only the leaves and blades of grass quivered for a moment. A polecat had caught a mouse. He now scurried off in another direction to enjoy his meal.

"What was that?" asked Bambi alarmed.

"Nothing," said his mother, calmly.

"But . . ." Bambi shivered, "but . . . I saw something there."

"Well, yes," said his mother, "don't be frightened. The polecat just killed a mouse."

But Bambi was terribly frightened. An unfamiliar and great fright gripped his heart. Many moments passed until he was able to speak again and then he asked, "Why did he kill the mouse?"

"Because . . ." His mother paused. ". . . let us go a bit faster now," she said then, as if she had just remembered something and she had forgotten his question. She started off. Bambi bounded after her.

There was a long pause; they again walked calmly and quietly. Finally, Bambi asked uneasily, "Will we kill a mouse, too, someday?"

"No," responded his mother.

"Never?" asked Bambi.

"Never ever," was her answer.

"Why not?" asked Bambi relieved.

"Because we do not kill anyone," said his mother simply.

Bambi was then cheerful again.

A loud shriek rang out from a small ash tree that stood next to the path. His mother continued on, paying it no notice. Curious Bambi, however, stopped in his tracks. Two roosters were quarreling about a nest they had looted in the branches above.

"Get lost! And never come back, you scoundrel!" called out one rooster to the other.

"Oh, don't you get yourself worked up, you fool," answered the other. "I am not afraid of you."

The first provoked again, "Go find your own nest, you thief! Why I'll crack your skull open!" He was outraged. "Such wickedness!" he bickered on, "such wickedness!"

The other noticed Bambi, fluttered and flew down a few branches and sneered at him, "And what are you looking at, you birdbrain? Get a move on!"

Aghast, Bambi bound off and quickly caught up to his mother who he then followed, well-behaved and startled, and thought that she might not have even noticed he was gone for a moment.

After some time, he inquired, "Mother... what is wickedness?"

His mother said, "I don't know."

Bambi considered this. Then he tried again. "Mother, why were those two so mean to each other?"

His mother answered, "They were quarreling over their food."

Bambi asked, "Will we ever fight that way over our food?"

"No," said his mother.

Bambi asked, "Why not?"

His mother responded, "There is enough for us all."

Bambi wanted to know something else, "Mother . . . ?"

"What is it?"

"Will we ever be so mean to each other?"

"No, my child," said his mother, "that is not how we are."

She continued on. Suddenly, it became bright before them, glaringly bright. The green jumble of bushes and shrubs fell away. They took just a few more steps and came out into the expansive freedom that opened before them. Bambi had the urge to jump out into the vast openness, but his mother stood still.

"What is this?" he asked impatiently and with fascination.

"The meadow," answered his mother.

"What is the meadow?" implored Bambi.

His mother cut his question short. "Soon you will find out for yourself." She had become stern and attentive. Motionless, she stood with her head held high, listening closely and checking the wind as she breathed out slowly.

"It is safe," she finally said, "we can go out."

Bambi bound forward, but she blocked his way. "You must wait until I call you." In an instant he became obediently silent and still.

"Very good," praised his mother. "And now pay very close attention and remember what I tell you." Bambi could hear the seriousness in his mother's voice and it made him tense.

"It is not that simple to just walk out into the meadow," his mother continued to explain. "It is a difficult and dangerous thing. Do not ask why. You will learn why some day. For now, just do exactly as I tell you. Will you?"

"Yes," promised Bambi.

"Very well. I will go out alone first. You will stand here and wait. And always watch me, keep an eye on me constantly. If you see that I turn back, then you must turn and run from here as fast as you can. I will come and find you then." She was silent as she seemed to consider what to say next and then urgently continued on, "No matter what, run, run as fast as you can. Run . . . even if something happens . . . even if you see that I . . . that I fall to the ground . . . you cannot stop for me, do you understand? Whatever you see or hear . . . just continue to run as fast and far from here as you can . . . ! Do you promise me this?"

"Yes," said Bambi quietly.

"When I call you, however," she continued on, "you may come. You can play on the meadow. It is lovely out there and you will enjoy it so. But . . . you must also promise me that at my first call, you will return to my side. Directly! Do you hear me?"

"Yes," said Bambi, even quieter this time. His mother spoke so severely.

She continued to talk again, "Out there on the meadow, when I call . . . you cannot dawdle or ask questions, you just run like the wind, back into the woods. No hesitating or pausing

. . . and should I begin to run then you too must do the same with all your might and you do not stop until we are back here in the forest. Will you forget what I have told you here?"

"No," said Bambi uneasily.

"I will go out there now," stated his mother and was calmer this time.

She stepped out. Bambi, who did not let his eyes off of her, saw that she slowly proceeded with cautious and high steps. Full of anticipation, fear, and curiosity, he stood there. He watched as she listened and looked in all directions; he saw she recoiled and he did the same, ready to jump back into the thicket at any time. Then his mother became calm again and after a minute had passed, she even became cheerful. She bowed her head briefly, straining her neck out, looked jovially at him and called, "Come out!"

Bambi leaped out. Such tremendous joy overtook him, with a magical power so that he had forgotten his fear in no time. In the thicket he just saw the green treetops above him, sometimes mixed with specks of blue here and there. Now he saw the entire vast blue sky which made him happy for a reason he did not even understand. In the forest, he only had known singular, broad beams of sunlight or the softly glowing splotches of light that hung, caught in branches. Now he suddenly found himself in the hot, blinding sun and felt its imposing power as it beamed down upon him and he stood in the midst of this glow, his eyes closed and his heart open. Bambi was in high spirits; he was beyond happy, it was simply amazing. Awkwardly, he leaped into the air three, four, five times on the spot where he stood. He could do nothing else; he had to. Something within him caused him to jump higher. His young limbs used all their power, he breathed so deeply and easily, and he drank in all the fragrances of the meadow breath with such enthusiasm that he had to jump again. Bambi was a child. Had he been a human, he would have let out a cheer. But he was a young deer, and deer could not cheer, at least not like human children do. Therefore, he cheered in his own way. With his legs and with his entire body, he went higher into the air.

His mother stood by and watched happily. She saw him frolicking with joy—jumping up and clumsily falling back to the same spot, looking about in stunned and bewildered amazement, before jumping up again a moment later. Again and again. She understood that Bambi had only known the small deer paths in the forest in his young life, and that he had was accustomed to living in the cramped thicket in the few short days since his birth and therefore he only moved in a small space, because he did not yet understand that he could move about and roam freely on the meadow. She crouched down low with her front legs, smiled in Bambi's direction for a moment, and then was off with such speed, dashing around in circles, and the high blades of grass just rustled about. Bambi was startled and stood still. Was this a sign that he should run back into the cover of the thicket? *"Do not worry about me,"* his mother had said, *"no matter what you hear or see, just run away, as quickly as possible!"* He wanted to turn back and flee, as he was told to do. Then suddenly his mother bounded over; in a wonderful rush she aimed back to where he stood, stopping two steps short of him, and again crouched down as before. She smiled and called out, "Come catch me!" and with a whoosh she was off again.

Bambi was baffled. What was going on? What had gotten into his mother all of a sudden? And then with such dizzying speed she was back again prodded Bambi's side with her nose and said hurriedly, "Oh come now, catch me!" and tore off again. Bambi stumbled after her for a few steps. Suddenly, his steps turned into bounds. His legs carried him, and his tempo grew smooth and natural so that he felt like he was flying. There was room enough beneath his hooves for him to bound further; there was room enough above him to leap higher and higher. Bambi was ecstatic. The grass whispered sweetly in his ears. It swept past his body, deliciously soft and delicate, like silk. His path curved and twisted, he darted in circles, turned about again, and charged forward. His mother stopped for a while, standing still to catch her breath and silently turned her head to watch Bambi race about.

Suddenly, Bambi could not run anymore. He slowed and walked daintily, pulling his legs up in high steps, to where his mother stood watching. Bambi looked at her happily. Then they continued on together, wandering side by side. Since he had come out of the woods, Bambi had only seen the sky, the sun, and the green expanse of the meadow with his body. With a dazed and muddled mind, he had seen the sky; with a comfortably sunned back and strengthening breaths, he had taken in the sun. Finally, he was now able to enjoy with his eyes—as with each moment he took in—and was overwhelmed by all the wonders and the glory of the meadow. Unlike in the forest, there was not a bare spot of soil. Each blade of grass had to fight for its tiny spot—nestled and swelled in lush splendor, bending to the side with each footstep only to spring up again, tall and proud. The wide green meadow was dotted with white daises, violets, the heavy heads of blooming clover, and the magnificent glowing golden buttons of dandelion heads in the air.

"Look there, mother," Bambi called, "a flower is flying away."

"That is not a flower," said his mother, "that is a butterfly."

Bambi looked at the butterfly with delight as it delicately took off from a stem and fluttered off, tumbling up and down through the air. Now Bambi saw that there were a great many butterflies in the air above the meadow. They all seemed to be in a rush yet were slow as they bobbed about. Watching them was a game that fascinated Bambi. It looked to him as if flowers—funny flowers—were wandering about and that they did not hold still on their stems but preferred to break away and dance a little. Or maybe they were flowers that were born to the earth with the morning sun and had not yet found a place, so they moved about fussily, searching, diving, and disappearing, only to reappear a moment later, a bit higher, to continue on their search, flying further and further because the best spots were already taken by other flowers.

Bambi watched all of them. He wished that one was closer to him so that he could examine it carefully, but alas they were far away. They crossed each other's paths, gliding about incessantly. He was confused watching them.

As he looked down at the ground in front of him, he was delighted to see a thousand kinds of vibrant life beneath him. It sprung and sprouted in all directions; its turmoil and bustle emerged only to sink away a moment later, back into the lush green from which it came.

"What is that, mother?" he asked

"Those are the children," answered his mother.

"Look over here," called Bambi, "there's a jumping piece of grass! Wow, look how high it can jump!"

"That isn't grass," explained his mother, "that is a little grasshopper."

"Why is it hopping around like that?" asked Bambi.

"Because we are walking here," answered his mother, ". . . it is afraid."

"Oh!" Bambi turned to the grasshopper that perched on an open, flat face of a daisy nearby.

"Oh," said Bambi politely, "you need not be afraid of us, we won't hurt you."

"I am not afraid," responded the grasshopper with a wavering voice. "I was just startled for a moment as I was talking with my wife just now."

"Excuse us, please," said Bambi. "We disturbed you."

"That is okay," rattled the grasshopper. "Since it's just you, it's alright. One just never knows who is coming, so one has to be careful."

"It happens to be my first very first time out in the meadow today," Bambi told him. "My mother was showing me . . ."

The stubborn grasshopper stood there and made a serious face and mumbled, "That really does not concern me. I don't have any time to chat with you, I have to find my wife! Hop!" and he was gone.

"Oh!" said Bambi taken aback and astounded by the height of the jump with which the grasshopper disappeared.

Bambi ran to his mother, "Mother . . . I was just speaking with him!"

"With whom?" asked his mother.

"With the grasshopper, of course" explained Bambi. "I was talking with him. He was so nice to me. And it looked so nice. It was a wonderful green, yet it was see-through at the end, unlike anything I have ever seen and so very fine!"

"Those are his wings."

"Really?" Bambi continued on. "It had such a serious face, so deep in thought. He was still nice to me, though. And oh, how he could jump! That must be terribly difficult. 'Hop,' he said and jumped up so high, I couldn't even see him go."

They went onward. The conversation with the grasshopper had excited Bambi and also made him a bit tired, as it was the first time that he had ever spoken to a stranger. He felt hungry and nuzzled up to his mother to refresh himself.

He then stood there quietly and daydreamed for a moment—in the gentle, sweet, drowsy sensation he felt each time he was fed by his mother. He noticed a light flower that was moving in the jumble of blades of grass. Bambi looked over more sharply. No, that wasn't a flower, it was a butterfly. Bambi carefully approached.

The butterfly hung heavy on a stalk and gently moved its wings.

"Please stay where you are!" Bambi called out to him.

"Why should I stay where I am? I am a butterfly, after all," answered the butterfly, amazed.

"Oh, stay here for a moment please!" Bambi pleaded, "I have wanted to see you up close for so long. Please be so kind."

"Fine," said the delicate cabbage white butterfly, "but not for too long."

Bambi stood in front of him. "How beautiful you are," called he out, charmed. "How exquisite! Like a flower!"

"What?" The butterfly flapped loudly with its wings. "Like a flower? Well, it is our opinion that we butterflies are more beautiful than the flowers."

Bambi was confused. "Of . . . of course," he stuttered, "much more beautiful . . . beg your pardon . . . I just meant to say . . ."

"It hardly matters to me what you meant to say," countered the butterfly. He arched his small body with an air of insolence and played vainly with his tender feelers.

Bambi watched him with fascination. "How dainty you are," he said. "How fine and dainty! And what splendid wings!"

The butterfly spread his wings wide apart and then brought them together tightly, so they resembled a tall, white sail.

"Oh," called Bambi, "now I see that you are more beautiful than the flowers. What's even more, you can fly! And flowers cannot do that. Because they grow in the ground, that's why."

The butterfly took off. "Enough," he said. "I can fly, indeed!" He then lifted off and took to the air with such unimaginable ease. His delicate white wings gently moved, full of grace, and he appeared to float on the sunny air. "Because of you I have stayed here, seated, for far too long," he said and fluttered up and down in front of Bambi, "but now I must fly on."

Such was the meadow.

CHAPTER 3

Deep in the thicket there was a small spot that belonged to Bambi's mother. It was just a few steps off the narrow path of the deer that ran through the forest, but it was impossible to find if one did not know the enclosure was within the thick bushes.

It was quite a narrow space, so narrow that Bambi and his mother hardly had much room left, and so low that Bambi's mother's head brushed up amongst the branches when she stood. Hazelnut, gorse, and dogwood branches grew so intertwined here in the thicket that very little light came down through the treetops. No sun fell on the forest floor here. This is where Bambi was born, and it was his and his mother's home.

His mother now lay nestled into the grass and slept. Even Bambi had snoozed for a moment. But now, he was suddenly wide awake. He stood up and looked around him.

Here within the forest, many shadows fell, and it was almost entirely dark. One could hear the forest rustling softly. Every now and then the titmice chirped, and here and there the bright laughter of a woodpecker or the joyless call of a crow sounded out. Otherwise, everything and every place far and wide was quiet. Only the still air boiled in the heat of noon, and it could be heard if one listened very closely. Here inside the thicket there was a dense, smothering heat.

Bambi looked down at his mother, "Are you sleeping?"

No, his mother was not asleep. She had awakened as soon as Bambi had stood up.

"What will we do now?" asked Bambi.

"Nothing," answered his mother, "we will stay here. Come, lay down once more and sleep."

But Bambi was not interested in sleeping. "Come," he pleaded, "come over to the meadow."

His mother lifted her head, "To the meadow? You want to go . . . to the meadow now . . . ?" She spoke so astounded, so full of dismay, that Bambi became afraid.

"Can we not go to the meadow now?" he asked shyly.

"No," his mother replied and sounded quite firm. "No, that's not possible now."

"Why not?" Bambi thought there was something strange going on. That made him even more afraid, but also more curious to find out more. "Why can't we go to the meadow now?"

"You will learn in time, when you are older . . ." his mother said, trying to satisfy his curiosity.

Bambi insisted, "Just tell me now."

"When you are older," repeated his mother. "You are just a young child now," she tenderly replied, "and this isn't the kind of thing for children to learn about." She then became quite stern. "Now, to go the meadow now . . . I cannot even imagine such a thing. In broad daylight!"

"But," argued Bambi, "when we were on the meadow just before, it was also daylight."

"That is something quite different," explained his mother, "it was early morning."

"Can we go only go out in the early morning?" Bambi was too curious now.

His mother had been patient. "Only in the early morning and the late evening . . . or at night . . ."

"And never during the day? Never ever . . . ?"

His mother hesitated for a moment. "Well, no," she finally replied, "sometimes . . . a few of us will go out together during the day. But only in special circumstances . . . I don't quite know how I should explain this all to you . . . you are too young to understand . . . some go . . . but they are then in the most danger . . ."

"But why are they in danger?" Bambi was now quite intrigued.

His mother was hesitant to say anything more about it. "Because they are just in danger . . . you see, my child, these are things that you simply cannot understand yet . . ."

Bambi thought that he could understand everything and that his mother did not want to give him a more honest answer. But he stayed silent.

"This is how we live," his mother continued to explain, "all of us. Even if we love the day . . . and we love the day, oh especially in our childhood . . . but still, we must be still during the day. From dusk till dawn we are able to roam about. Do you understand that?"

"Yes."

"Well then, my child, you understand now why we must stay here where we are. Here we are safe. And now, lay down again and sleep."

But Bambi did not want to lay down now. "Why are we safe here?" he asked.

"Because all the branches watch over us, because all the twigs of the bushes crackle, because fallen dry brush on the ground cracks to warn us, because the withered leaves of the years past now lay on the ground and rustle to give us a sign . . . because the jay is there and the magpies as well; they all keep watch, and this way we will know when someone comes from afar.

"What is that," inquired Bambi, "'leaves of the years past'?"

"Come now, lay down next to me," said his mother. "I will tell you now." Bambi willingly sat down next to his mother and nestled up to her and she told him that the trees did not always stay green, that the sun and its beautiful warmth disappears. Then it would turn cold. The leaves would turn yellow, then brown and red from the frost, before slowly falling off, leaving the trees and bushes to stretch their bare branches to the sky, looking exhausted and poor. The withered leaves would lay strewn about the ground, and when a foot would touch them, they would rustle, *Someone is coming.* Oh, how good they are, the withered leaves of the years past. They protect us well, so diligent and vigilant they are. Now, in the middle of the summer, many of them are hiding under the young growth of the ground cover and warn us of every danger from a distance.

Bambi pressed himself tightly against his mother. He forgot the meadow. It was so comfortable to sit and listen to his mother.

As his mother became silent, he thought. He thought it was very kind of the good, old leaves that they would so dutifully keep watch, even though they were withered and frozen and had already gone through so much. He considered what the danger his mother always referred to could possibly be.

But thinking this much was making him tired. It was so quiet all around him, the only sound was the wind. And so, he fell fast asleep.

CHAPTER 4

One night, as he stepped out into the meadow with his mother, he thought that he had seen and heard everything there was to see and hear on the meadow. But it turned out that he did not know of all the things in life, as he had assumed.

At first it was just like any other time. Bambi played catch with his mother. He ran about in circles; the wide openness, the high heavens, and the fresh air filled him with a feeling of freedom and joy, so he sped faster and faster. After a while, he noticed that his mother was standing still. He clumsily came to an abrupt stop. He stopped so suddenly, that his legs splayed out wide apart. He couldn't pull them back together, so he had to jump up, high into the air, in order to land standing straight. His mother stood a ways away and appeared to be speaking with someone, but he couldn't tell who it could be from where he was standing, with all that high grass between them. Bambi wandered closer out of curiosity. In front of his mother, amidst the jumble of straw and grass, were two long ears. They were a grey-brown color with smart, small black stripes. Bambi stopped short, but his mother called to him, "Come over here. This is our friend, Rabbit . . . now, come already. Let him see you."

Bambi walked up close. There sat a decent looking rabbit. His long ears rose up mighty high and then fell down again, as if suddenly worn out. Bambi was a little alarmed by the imposing mustache he saw when he stared closely at the rabbit's face. But he noticed that the rabbit had a very gentle face, very kind features, and that he looked bashfully at the world through his big, round eyes. He truly looked like a friend, the rabbit did. Bambi's fleeting concern disappeared immediately. Strangely, he even lost all fear he had initially felt for the rabbit, and instead he felt familiar.

"Good evening, young sir," greeted Friend Rabbit with exquisite politeness.

Bambi could only nod back. "Good evening." He didn't know why but he nodded again. It was very friendly, very kind, but a little cold. This was his nature—how he was born.

"What a handsome young prince!" said Friend Rabbit to Bambi's mother. He looked attentively at Bambi, lifting one of his tall ears, then slowly the second one, holding them high, but sometimes letting them quickly fall back down, which Bambi did not like. This gesture seemed to mean *"it's not quite worth the trouble."*

Meanwhile, Friend Rabbit continued to gaze gently at Bambi with his large, round eyes. His nose and his mouth, hidden by the magnificent mustache, moved incessantly—as someone who is holding back a sneeze may twitch their nose and lips. Bambi laughed. Friend Rabbit immediately joined him in laughter, so easily, and his eyes became more thoughtful.

"I congratulate you," he said to Bambi's mother, "I sincerely congratulate you, what a fine son. Yes, yes, yes . . . what a magnificent prince he will be . . . yes, yes, yes, you can see this kind of thing in someone."

He then adjusted himself, pulling his body upright, and sat upon his hind legs, which baffled Bambi beyond measure. After he had looked Bambi over entirely, twitching his great nose, he dropped back down to sit on all fours again. "Yes, now I must insist to the revered gentlemen," he said, "that I continue on, as I still have many things to do this evening . . . humbly, I excuse myself." He turned and hopped away, ears pressed back into his shoulders.

"Good evening," Bambi called out after him.

His mother smiled, "Our good friend Rabbit . . . so kind and modest. He has not had a simple life." There was sympathy in her words.

Bambi wandered around and left his mother to her meal. He hoped to meet his acquaintances from the first visit to the meadow, and he was also anxious to make new friends. He did not know it, for he did not understand it, but he longed for friend. Suddenly, he heard a faint noise from far away in the meadow, and felt a soft, rapid knocking up through the ground. He looked up. Over there, at the other edge of the forest, something scurried across the grass. A creature . . . no, wait . . . two! Bambi glanced over to his mother, but she was unconcerned; she seemed to not have even noticed it with her head so far in the grass. There it was again, running around as if hunting in circles, just as he had done before, circling about. Bambi was so confused that he took a step backwards, ready to bolt. That caught his mother's attention and she raised her head.

"What is it?" she called.

But Bambi was speechless; he found no words and stammered, "There . . . over there . . ."

His mother looked over in the direction of his gaze. "Oh that," she said, "that is my cousin, and ah, look, she has a child now . . . no, wait she has two." His mother had spoken with such cheer, but now she was serious, "No . . . that Ena would have two children . . . really, two . . . !"

Bambi stood and stared. In the distance he could now make out a figure that resembled his mother. He had never before seen something similar to her. He saw the figure walking through the grass in figure eights, but only its red back was visible in thin red stripes amongst the grass.

"Come," said his mother, "we should go over. A bit of company would be good for you."

Bambi wanted to run over, but as his mother went very slowly and with each step, looked about carefully, Bambi restrained himself. But he felt the fiercest excitement and was very impatient.

His mother spoke again. "I thought that we would find Ena here someday. *'Where is she?'* I often thought to myself. I knew that she had a child, too, well that was easy to guess. But two children . . ."

They had long been noticed by the others who now came to meet them. Bambi ought to have greeted his aunt, but he could not take his eyes off her children.

His aunt was very kind. "Yes," she spoke to him, "this is Gobo, and this is Faline. You can always play with each other."

The children stood stiff and still, staring at each other. Gobo stood close to Faline, and Bambi stood across from them. No one moved. They stood and stared.

"Oh, let them be," said his mother, "they will become friends soon enough."

"What a beautiful child," responded Aunt Ena, "truly beautiful and so strong . . . such poise."

"Well, he is kind" said his mother modestly. "One must be grateful. But that you now have two children, Ena . . ."

"Yes, oh well, sometimes it's this way, sometimes it's that

way," explained Ena. "You know, my dear, I have had children before . . ."

His mother said, "Bambi is my first . . ."

"You see," Ena consoled her, "maybe that will change for you soon enough . . ."

The children still stood there, observing each other. No one said a word. Suddenly, Faline sprung forward and darted off. This standing and staring was just too boring.

Bambi followed her instantly. Gobo took up after him. They took off, making crescent shapes, turning at lightning speed, tumbling over each other, and chasing wildly about. It was splendid. When they stopped, abruptly and breathless, they already felt quite familiar with each other. They began to chat.

Bambi told them about the kind grasshopper and the butterfly he had spoken to.

"Did you speak with the beetle, too?" asked Faline.

No, Bambi had not spoken to the beetle. He had not seen her; he did not even know who that was.

"I talk with her a lot," Faline explained, a bit proudly.

"The jay scolded me," said Bambi.

"Really?" Gobo was surprised. "Was the jay really that sassy to you?" Gobo was easily amazed, and also easily surprised, and he was not always very modest.

"Well," he continued, "the hedgehog poked me in the nose." He mentioned this causally.

"Who is the hedgehog?" inquired Bambi happily. It was so wonderful to stand here, with friends, and to hear such exciting things.

"The hedgehog is a terrible creature," declared Faline. "Such long spines all over its entire body . . . and they're also quite mean!"

"Do you really thing that he is mean?" asked Gobo. "He never hurts a soul."

"Oh?" Faline quickly retorted, "did he not poke you?"

"Ah, come, that was just because I wanted to speak with him," objected Gobo, "and it was just a little poke. It didn't really hurt much."

Bambi turned to Gobo, "Why didn't he want to speak with you?"

"He doesn't like to speak with anyone," interjected Faline. "As soon as anyone gets close to him, he rolls up in a ball and all you see are his spines. Our mother said he is the kind of creature we don't want to play with."

Gobo thought aloud, "Maybe he is just afraid."

But Faline understood this kind of thing better, "Our mother said that you shouldn't get involved with someone like that."

Bambi quietly said to Gobo, "Do you know what danger is?"

All three suddenly were serious, and they all bent their heads close together to speak privately.

Gobo thought for a moment. He sincerely tried to think of what it could be, as he could see how curious Bambi was, waiting for an answer.

"Danger . . ." he whispered, "danger . . . is something quite terrible . . ."

"Yes," said Bambi urgently, "something quite terrible indeed . . . but what?"

They were trembling with terror.

Suddenly, Faline called out, loud and happy, "Danger . . . is when you have to run away . . ." She immediately jumped away—she didn't want to stand there and be afraid. Bambi and Gobo jumped after her. They all began to play again, bounding through the green, glistening, silky meadow and had soon all but forgotten the serious question. After a while they paused and stood together, as before, to chat. They looked over at their mothers. They were still standing happily together, eating a little and talking calmly in hushed voices.

Aunt Ena lifted her head and called over to her children, "Gobo! Faline! It is almost time to go . . ."

Bambi's mother also urged him, "Come now, it is time."

"Oh, a bit longer," pleaded Faline frantically, "just a little bit longer."

Bambi pleaded, "Let's stay! Please! It is so lovely!"

Even the typically shy Gobo called out, "Oh, please it is so lovely . . . just a little longer."

All three continued to speak all at once.

Ena looked at his mother, "Well, didn't I say so? Now we won't be able to get them apart."

Something else happened in this moment and it was bigger and more magnificent than all the other things that Bambi had experienced today.

From within the forest came a tapping, pounding sound that vibrated through the ground. Branches cracked, twigs rustled, and before the deer could prick up their ears, something burst out of the thicket. The first one came out rushing and stamping about, the other came up behind with a ruckus. They raced out like the winds of a great storm, made a wide arc in the meadow, then dove back into the forest from where they came; all that then remained was the sound of their galloping. Then again, they came roaring out of the thicket once more and suddenly stood still, twenty paces apart.

Bambi looked at both of them and did not move. The two looked like Mother and Aunt Ena. But upon their heads glinted a crown of antlers with rich brown pearls and bright white prongs. Bambi was quite stunned; he looked from one to the other. One was shorter, and his crown was smaller. But the other one was beyond beautiful. He carried his head high, and the crown was perched very high on his head. It sparkled both dark and light, adorned with the splendor of many black and brown pearls and with broad, shimmering white ends.

"Oh!" gasped Faline in amazement. Gobo repeated quietly, "Oh!" Bambi however said nothing. He was enraptured and stunned, silent.

Now they both moved and turned away from each other, each in a different direction, and then slowly walked back into the forest. The meadow edge was very close to the children, Bambi's mother, and Aunt Ena. As he passed before them in silent splendor, he carried his regal head with its noble crown high and straight and paid no attention to anyone. The children did not dare breathe until he vanished in the thicket. They looked after the others and just in that moment, the great arches of tree boughs closed behind him.

Faline was the first to break the silence. "Who was that?" she asked. Her small, determined voice wavered.

Hardly audible, Gobo repeated the refrain, "Who was that?"

Bambi was silent.

Aunt Ena announced with a festive tone, "Those were the fathers."

Nothing more was said, and all went their own ways.

Aunt Ena went off with her children, behind the nearest bush. That was their path. Bambi had to cross the wide meadow to the oak to get to their path. Bambi stayed silent for some time. Finally, he asked, "Did they not see us?"

His mother understood what he meant and said, "Of course they did. They see everything."

Bambi felt anxious; he was too shy to ask questions but felt the urge to ask within him. He continued, "... Why ... ?" and fell silent once more.

His mother coaxed him, "What do you want to say, my child?"

"Why did they not stay with us?"

"They do not stay with us," answered his mother, "just sometimes . . ."

Bambi probed further, "Why did they not speak with us?"

His mother said, "Now they did not speak with us, just sometimes . . . You must wait until they come, and you must wait for them to speak . . . when they want to."

A stormy feeling swelled in Bambi. "Will my father speak with me?"

"Of course, my child," promised his mother, "when you are older, he will speak with you and you will also be with him sometimes."

Bambi continued to walk in silence alongside his mother, all of his senses were overwhelmed with the appearance of the Father. *"How magnificent he is!"* He thought over and over, *"How magnificent he is!"*

As if his mother could hear his thoughts, she spoke, "If you grow as old as he, my child—if you are smart and stay away from danger—then you will also be as strong and magnificent as your father, and you will also wear a crown such as his."

Bambi took a deep breath in. His heart blossomed with happiness and apprehension.

CHAPTER 5

Time passed, and Bambi learned from his many adventures and hundreds of experiences. Sometimes he became upset at the thought that he still had so much to learn.

He had become better at listening. Not just listening at what happens close by—the kind of sound that hits your ears on its own. No, that is hardly a real art form. Rather, he could listen so closely, listen to everything that stirs so softly, to every fine crackle the wind carries with it. He knew, for example, if there was a pheasant running through the bushes; he knew the delicate tripping through the leaves and its pattern of starts and stops. He could even recognize the sound of wood mice as they ran back and forth along their short paths. Then the moles: he knew when they were in a good mood and chasing each other under an elderberry bush that rustled just so. He knew the audacious, bright call of the hawks, and could hear the difference in their tone when angry that another hawk or an eagle had come along, and they feared their territory may be taken from them. He knew the flapping of the pigeon's wings; and the beautiful, distant hiss of a duck flapping; and so many more forest sounds.

He also gradually learned how to sniff things out. Soon, he would be as good as his mother. He drew in the air and picked apart all the scents.

"Oh, that's clover and meadow grass," he would think to himself when the wind blew in from the meadow. *"Yes, and Friend Rabbit is also out there; I know the scent well."* Then again, in the midst of the odors of leaves, earth, leeks, and woodruff, he would realize that somewhere the polecat was passing by; he recognized, when he stuffed his nose down into the dirt and thoroughly examined it, if the fox had been there; or he would notice, *"My relatives are here, somewhere nearby, Aunt Ena with the children."*

He was now completely familiar with the night and he no longer yearned to run about during the daytime. Happily, he spent the daytime in the small, shady den of foliage with his mother. He heard the air boil with heat, and he slept. From time to time he would wake up, listen closely, and sense that everything was as it should be. Everything was OK. Only the tiny titmice chattered a little; the warblers, who can almost never keep quiet, spoke; and the pigeons did not cease with their enthusiastic, endearing calls. What about their calls could concern him? He'd simply fall back to sleep.

In fact, the night now pleased him very much. Everything was lively, everything in motion. Of course, one must be cautious at night, but one was without worry and free to roam about. And everywhere one went, one met acquaintances who were also more carefree than usual. At night, the forest was solemn and quiet. There were only a few voices that became loud in this silence, but they sounded different from the voices of the day, and they made a stronger impression. Bambi liked to listen to the Owl. She had such a distinguished flight—so silent, so light. A butterfly made no more noise than she did, and she was so terrifically tall. She also had such a meaningful face—so determined, so thoughtful—and she had astounding eyes. Bambi admired her firm, calm, brave gaze. He enjoyed listening when she spoke to his mother or to someone else. Often, he stood a back a bit, just a little afraid of the commanding gaze that he admired so much—and yet there were so many wise things she said that he could not understand. But he knew that they were clever things that charmed him and filled him with adoration for the Owl. Then the Owl would begin her song. "Haa-ah–hahaha–haa-ah!" she sang. It sounded different from the song of the thrush or the oriole, quite unlike the friendly motto of the cuckoo, but oh how Bambi loved the song of the Owl. He felt a mysterious seriousness from it—an unspeakable wisdom and a melancholy.

Then there was the Tawny Owl, a fascinating little fellow. Clever, merry, and exceptionally curious, he was always intent to cause a stir. "Uj-iik! Uj-iik!" His cry would ring out in a shocking, terribly shrill voice. It sounded as if he was in fear for his life. But indeed, he was in a brilliant mood and was most thrilled when he had frightened someone. "Uj-iik!" he would cry out, so terribly loud that one could hear it in the forest from a great distance. But hidden within his call was a soft, cooing laughter, and one could only hear it up close. Bambi had come to the conclusion that the Tawny Owl rejoiced when it frightened someone, or when someone thought something bad had happened to him. Since realizing this, Bambi had never, when close by, failed to rush in and ask, "Did something happen to you?" Or he'd say with a sigh, "Oh my, how startled I was just now!" Then the Tawny Owl would be amused. "Yes, yes," he would say with a laugh, "it sounds quite wretched." He'd puff up his feathers, looking like a soft, grey ball, and would be charmingly pretty.

There had also been a few storms, both during the day and night. The first one came during the day, and Bambi felt more and more anxious as it became darker and darker in his small den of foliage. It felt as if the night had suddenly fallen from the sky in the middle of the day. Then, as the storm roared through the forest and the silent trees began to moan aloud, Bambi began to tremble with fear. When the lightning flashed and the thunder crashed, Bambi was beside himself, believing that the world would be torn to pieces. He ran after his mother—who had jumped up—somewhat confused and was now pacing back and forth in the thicket. He could not think, could not believe what was happening. Then the rain came and fell in furious downpours. Every creature in the forest had crept off, the forest was empty, but there was little shelter from the rain. Even the thickest shrubbery could not protect you from the lashing of the rushing water. But the lightning stopped, its fiery beam no longer flaring through the treetops; the thunder became distant until it was just a far-away murmur, and soon it stopped completely. Now the rain became gentler. Its broad hum sounded steadily and strong for another hour; the forest stood, deeply breathing in the calm and letting the rain pour over it, and no one was afraid any longer. This feeling had vanished; the rain had washed it away.

Bambi's mother had never taken him to the meadow as early as on this day. It was not even evening. The sun still stood high in the sky, and the air was powerfully fresh; it smelled stronger than usual. The forest sang with a thousand voices, for all the creatures had emerged from their hiding places and now hurried about, telling each other what they had experienced.

Before they arrived at the meadow, they came past the big oak tree, just on the edge of the forest, close to their path. They always had to pass this beautiful, tall tree when they went to meadow. Now the Squirrel sat on a branch and greeted them. Bambi enjoyed their serene friendship and the first time they had met, he had mistaken him for a very small deer on account of his red coat and had stared at him in astonishment. But Bambi was really too innocent at the time and just did not understand everything there is to understand. Right from the beginning he had taken an exceptional liking to Squirrel. He was so well-mannered, so pleasantly talkative, and Bambi was amused by how wonderfully he could tumble, climb, jump, and balance. As they chatted, Squirrel ran up and down the smooth tree trunk as if it was nothing at all. Then he sat upright on a swaying branch, leaning comfortably against his bushy tail, which rose gracefully behind him, showed his white chest, fussed daintily with his small forepaws, turned his head back and forth, laughed with his cheerful eyes, and told so many jokes and interesting tales. Now he came down again, so fast and with such great bounds that one would think he was about to fall on your head. He waved his long red tail vigorously and greeted from high above, "Good day! Good day! Nice of you to come by!"

Bambi and his mother stopped for a moment.

Squirrel ran down the smooth tree trunk. "Well," he chatted merrily, ". . . seems you faired the storm well? Yes, I see that everything is in best form. That is the most important thing." He ran as fast as lightning back up the tree trunk and spoke all the while, "No, it is much too wet down there for me. You wait, and I will look for a spot that is better for me. I hope that doesn't bother you? Thank you! Oh, I didn't think it would bother you. We can continue our conversation from here, too."

He ran the length of a branch, back and forth. "What a show that was," he continued on. "Such a loud fuss! Well, you can imagine how scared I was. It is best to hide somewhere in a cranny, hardly daring to move. That is the worst of it, really, to sit there so still and not move. With the hopes that nothing will happen, and well, my tree is excellent for such cases; no, there is nothing that can happen to it. My tree is excellent . . . I must say that. I am quite pleased. No matter how far I explore, I have never found another one I would want. But oh, when it starts to pour like that, I can't help but simply get excited all over again . . ."

The squirrel sat still for a moment, leaning against his beautiful, towering tail, exposing his white chest, and pressing both front paws sentimentally to his heart. It was easy to tell he had been upset by the storm.

"We just were on our way to the meadow now," said Bambi's mother, "to dry ourselves in the sun."

"Oh, that is a splendid idea," called out the Squirrel. "How smart you are, truly; I am always saying how smart you are!" With that, he jumped up to a higher branch. "There is nothing finer you could do right now than to go out on to the meadow," he called down from above. Then he jumped, zig-zagging his way through the treetops with light, effortless leaps. "I also want to go up high enough where I have sun," he chattered on happily. "After such a storm, we all are completely drenched! I will go all the way up now!" It did not matter if anyone was still listening.

The meadow was quite full of life. Friend Rabbit was sitting there with his family. Aunt Ena stood there along with her children and a few other familiar faces. Today Bambi even saw the fathers again. They came slowly out of the forest, one from this side, the other from that side; there was even a third one that appeared. Slowly, they walked up and down along the edge of the forest in formation, each standing in their own place. They paid no attention to anyone, they did not even speak to each other. Bambi often looked over at them, respectful and full of curiosity.

Then he spoke with Faline and Gobo, and with a few other children. He thought they might be able to play a bit. Everyone agreed and so they began to bound about in circles. Faline appeared to be the happiest of them all. She was so refreshed and nimble, bubbling forth with sudden ideas. But Gobo soon became tired. The storm had frightened him terribly; he could still feel his heart racing, even now. Gobo was generally a bit weaker, but Bambi loved him because he was so good and so eager, and always a bit sad, though he tried to not let it show.

CHAPTER 6

Time passed, and Bambi learned how delicious the grass of the meadow tastes, how delicate the buds are, and how sweet the clover is. When he would beg his mother for milk, she would often turn him away. "You're not a child anymore," she would say. Sometimes she would even say, quite directly, "Go on now, leave me alone." She would even stand up in their small forest den, awakening in the middle of the day, and leave without paying any attention if Bambi followed her or not. Sometimes it also seemed as if his mother would pay no mind—as they wandered along their usual paths—if Bambi was in tow or lagging behind. One day, Bambi awoke and his mother was gone. Bambi was not sure how it could be; he had no explanation. But his mother was gone, and Bambi was alone for the first time.

He was surprised; he grew restless, then nervous, and began to yearn pitifully for her. He stood there in sadness and called out. No one replied, no one came.

He listened closely, he tried to sense something, but there was not a trace he could smell. Nothing. Again, he called out.

Now, quietly, timid and imploringly, he called out after her "Mother . . . Mother . . . !" all in vain.

Despair overwhelmed him; he couldn't stand it anymore and decided to leave.

He wandered the paths that he knew well, stopping here and there to call out, then walking on again with hesitant steps, fearful and confused. He was very sad.

He continued on and on, eventually reaching paths he had never walked before—he came to areas that were strange to him. He did not know these places or where he was.

Then he heard two children's voices that called out as he did, "Mother . . . Mother . . . !"

He stood still and listened.

"Can it be that that is Gobo and Faline? It must be them."

Quickly, he followed their voices and soon saw their red coats shimmering through the leaves. Gobo and Faline. There they stood gloomily beside each other under a dogwood and called out, "Mother . . . Mother . . . !"

They were excited when they heard something stirring in the brush. When they recognized Bambi, however, they looked disappointed. Nevertheless, they were a little happy to see it was him. And Bambi was glad to no longer be so alone.

"My mother is gone," Bambi said.

"Ours is too," answered Gobo feebly.

They all look at each other and were quite upset.

"Wherever could they be?" asked Bambi. He held back a sob.

"I don't know," sighed Gobo. His heart was racing again, and he felt quite distressed.

Suddenly, Faline spoke up, "I think . . . they are with the fathers . . ."

Gobo and Bambi looked shocked. Their faces changed, awestruck. "Do you think? With the fathers?" asked Bambi as a shiver ran along his back.

Faline also shivered, but she made a meaningful face. She behaved like someone who knows more than they are willing to tell. Of course, she was not certain. She wasn't even sure where the notion came from. Once again, Gobo repeated the question, "Do you really think so?" and she made a smart expression and again repeated mysteriously, "Yes, I do think so."

It was no more than a guess and left a lot to the imagination. Nevertheless, it did not calm Bambi. He could hardly even think, he was so excited and sad.

He wandered off. He did not like to stay in one spot for so long. Faline and Gobo accompanied him a bit; all three called out together, "Mother . . . Mother . . . !" This time it was Gobo and Faline who stopped; they dared not continue. Faline said, "Why should we go further? Our mother knows where we are. We should stay here so that she can find us when she comes back."

Bambi went off on his own. He wandered through a thicket and found himself in a small opening. In the middle of the opening, Bambi stood still. Suddenly, it was as if he were fixed to this spot and could not move.

There, on the edge of the opening, stood a figure in the high hazel bushes. Bambi had never seen such a figure before. At the same time, he smelled a scent—something carried on the air—that he had never smelled before. It was a strange odor, heavy and sharp, exciting and maddening.

Bambi stared at the figure. It was strangely erect, peculiarly slender, and had a pale face that was naked around its eyes and nose. Ghastly naked. The face gave him horrible sense of dread with its icy stare. This face seemed to have the tremendous power to paralyze. It was tormentingly unbearable to look at, yet Bambi stood there and stared at it, unable to look away.

The figure stayed still for some time, showing no emotion. Then it stretched out a leg—one that sat up high, close to its face. Bambi had not even noticed there was a leg there. But as it stretched this terrible leg out into the air, it was as if the mere gesture had swept Bambi out of its way, like a down feather in the wind. In no time, Bambi found himself back in the thicket where he came from. He had fled.

All of a sudden, his mother was there again. She jumped out from bushes and flowers, landing next to him. They both ran on quickly. His mother lead, as she knew the way, and Bambi followed. In this formation they ran until they reached their den.

"Did you . . . see it?" asked his mother quietly. Bambi could not answer; he was out of breath. All he could do was nod.

"That . . . was . . . Him!" said his mother.

They both shuddered.

CHAPTER 7

Bambi often spent time alone. Now he was not as afraid as he had been the first times. His mother would disappear, and he could call as much as he liked, but she would not come. Yet suddenly, she would reappear.

One night, he was again wandering about all by himself. Not even Gobo and Faline could find him. The sky was beginning to turn pale grey, and dusk began to fall, making the vaulting treetops above visible through the undergrowth of the shrubs. There was a rustling in the bushes, and a gust blew through the drifting leaves. Then out of nowhere appeared his mother, dashing by. Close on her heels came another sweeping figure. Bambi could not make out who it had been. Aunt Ena or his father, or maybe someone else. He had recognized his mother immediately, even though she had passed him so quickly. He had heard her voice. She screamed, but it seemed to Bambi that it might be a joke. Still, he noticed a touch of fear in in her voice.

Another time, something happened, but it was daytime. Bambi had made his way through the thickets for hours and hours. Finally, he began to call out. Not necessarily because he was worried. He just did not want to be so alone anymore and felt that he would soon feel miserable. So, he began to call out for his mother.

Suddenly, one of the old bucks stood in front of him and looked at him with a stern gaze. Bambi had not heard him coming and he was startled. The buck was more imposing to look at than the other fathers, taller and prouder. His coat was a deep, deep blush red, but his face already shimmered silver-gray, and mightily atop his head sat a tall, black-bejeweled crown between his ears. "Why are you calling?" asked the old buck with a harsh voice. Bambi trembled with awe and did not dare answer. "Your mother does not have time for you right now!" he continued on. Bambi was defeated by this commanding voice, but at the same time he admired it. "Can you not be alone? Shame on you!" Bambi wanted to say that he was very good at being alone, that he often was left alone, but he could not manage to speak. He listened obediently and was terribly ashamed of himself. The old buck turned around and left. Bambi did not know why or where he went—did not know if he had gone quickly or slowly. He had just left, as suddenly as he had come. Bambi listened intently for a sign, but he heard no footstep fading away, heard no movement. He thought, therefore, that the old buck might still be very near, and sniffed at the air in all directions. It brought no clue. Bambi breathed a sigh of relief to be alone once more, but he felt a strong desire to see the buck again and to gain his approval.

When his mother did come, he did not tell her about his encounter. He also stopped calling after her so much when she would leave. He thought of the buck when he wandered by himself; he wished so intently to cross paths with him again. Then he would tell him, *"See, I don't call out any more,"* and the buck would praise him.

He did tell Gobo and Faline the next time they were on the meadow together. They listened intently and had never encountered something like that themselves. "Were you not afraid?" asked Gobo excitedly. Oh yes! Bambi admitted that he had been afraid. Just a little. "I would have been dreadfully afraid," declared Gobo. Bambi replied, no, he had not been so afraid, since the old buck had been magnificent. Gobo said, "Oh that would not have helped me much. I would not even have been able to look at him, that's how scared I would have been. When I get afraid, my eyes flicker and my fear blinds me, and my heart beats so hard that I cannot breathe." Faline had been silent and lost in thought as Bambi told his story.

The next time they saw each other, Gobo and Faline came over in a great rush of excitement. They were alone again, as was Bambi. "We have been looking everywhere for you," called Gobo.

"Yes," said Faline with a tone of importance, "because we just found out exactly who it was that you saw in the woods."

Bambi jumped with curiosity. "Who . . . !?"

Faline said solemnly, "It was the Old One, the great, old Crown Prince."

"How do you know that?" demanded Bambi.

"Our mother told us!" replied Faline.

Bambi was amazed. "Did you tell her the story?" They both nodded. "It was supposed to be a secret!" Bambi said, outraged.

Gobo didn't hesitate, "I didn't tell. Faline did."

But Faline retorted cheerfully, "I say, a secret! I wanted to know who it was. Now we know and that is much more interesting!" Bambi was eager to hear everything and was satisfied with all Faline shared. "He is the noblest creature in the whole forest. He is the great, old Crown Prince. There is no one equal to him. Nobody knows how old he is. Nobody knows where he lives. Nobody calls him their kin. Few have ever seen him. Sometimes it was said that he had died, because he had not been seen for so long. Then he appeared again, so it was then known that he is still alive. No one ever dared ask him where he goes. He speaks with no one and no one dares speak with him. He walks paths that no one else walks; he knows the forest as far as it reaches. For him there is no danger. The other princes sometimes fight among themselves—sometimes only for fun or competition, sometimes in seriousness. But nobody has fought with him for many years. Those who used to fight with him a long time ago, none of them are alive. He is the great Crown Prince."

Bambi forgave Gobo and Faline for spilling his secret to their mother. He was just happy to have learned such important things. But he was also glad that Gobo and Faline did not know everything. That the great Crown Prince had said, "Can't you be alone?" That he had said, "Shame on you!" They did not know these things. Bambi was glad that he kept these words to himself. Faline would have told this secret all the same and then the whole forest would have gossiped about it.

That evening, as the moon rose, Bambi's mother came back once again. All of a sudden, she appeared under the big oak tree at the edge of the meadow and looked around for Bambi. He noticed her immediately and ran to her. That night Bambi again experienced something new. His mother was tired and hungry, so they did not wander as far as usual. His mother sat in the grass to eat her meal that night, in the same spot where Bambi used to eat most of his meals. Together they grazed on the bushes, wandering further and further into the forest as they ate. There was a big rushing noise in the bushes. Before Bambi knew what was happening, his mother began to yell loudly as she was prone to do when she was very frightened or confused. *"A-oh!"* she shouted, leaping, stopping and shouting, *"A-oh, ba-oh!"* Bambi now saw it—tremendous phantoms passing in the great rush. They came very close. They resembled Bambi and his mother, resembled Aunt Ena and all the rest of his kin, but they were gigantic in their form, so immense that he had to look up at them—he felt overwhelmed. Bambi also began to wail. *"A-oh . . . Ba-oh . . . Ba-oh!"* He was not even aware he was wailing, he could not help it. The long herd of these phantoms was steadily rushing by. Three, four gigantic shapes in a row. Finally, one which was taller than the rest passed, with a wild mane on his head and a whole tree as a crown. It was breathtaking to see him. Bambi stood there and bawled with all his might, for it was the eeriest thing he had ever seen. He was afraid, indeed, but in a different way. He felt pathetically small, and even his mother seemed pitifully meager. He was ashamed, without knowing why, but at the same time the horror rattled him, and he began to paw at the dirt. *"Ba-oh . . . Ba-a-oh!"* he called, letting out his fear through his wailing.

The herd had passed. There was nothing left to see or hear of them. His mother was still silent. Bambi however blurted out from time to time. He was still so full of energy.

"Be quiet now," said his mother. "They have left us."

"Oh, mother," Bambi whispered at first, "what was that?"

"Well, they generally are not harmful," his mother spoke slowly, "they are our large relatives . . . you see . . . they are large and noble . . . much more noble than us."

"Are they not dangerous?" asked Bambi.

"No, usually not," explained his mother. "Of course, there have been accidents. There are stories of accidents, but stories are just talk and I do not know if there is any truth in these stories. They've never done anything to me, or nobody else that I know."

"Why would they want to do something to us," asked Bambi, "if they are our relatives?" He wanted to be calm and quiet, but he was still shivering.

"No, they would not harm us," answered his mother, "but I don't know, I just get startled each time I see them. I can hardly believe it, every time I feel this way."

Bambi was gradually pacified by this conversation, but he remained deep in his thoughts. Just above him, in the branches of an alder, was perched an owl that hooted spectacularly. But Bambi was absent-minded and forgot to even pretend to be frightened. Still the Tawny Owl came over and inquired, "Did I scare you?"

"But of course," answered Bambi, "You always startle me so."

The Tawny Owl laughed quietly to himself; he was pleased with this answer. "Hopefully you will not hold it against me," he said, "that is just how I am." He puffed himself up so that he looked like a round ball, buried his beak into the fluffy plumage, and made a pleased, yet serious face. He was very satisfied with himself.

Bambi poured out his heart to the owl, "Did you know," he began cautiously, "I just had quite the scare, an even bigger one."

"Is that so?" asked the Tawny Owl, dissatisfied.

Bambi told him of the encounter with the large relatives.

"Ah, come, stop with stories of your relatives," snipped the Tawny Owl. "I have relatives, too, you know. All I do is show up somewhere and they all start in on me. No, relatives are really of no use. If they are larger than we are, they are good for nothing. If they are smaller than us, they are good for even less. If they are larger than we are, then we can hardly stand them, because they are so proud, and if they are smaller than we are, then they can hardly stand us, because they are so proud to be small and cannot stand it if we are the proud ones. No, I don't want to deal with any of the lot."

"But, you see . . . I don't know my relatives at all . . ." said Bambi, his voice hinted he was shy and wistful. "I had never heard of them and today was the first time I even saw them."

"Oh, you pay no mind to them," the Tawny Owl advised him. "You believe me," he rolled his eyes with great significance. "Believe me, yes, that is the best way. Relatives are never as good as friends. You see, take us for example. We are not relatives, but we are good friends and that is quite pleasant."

Bambi wanted to say one more thing, but the Tawny Owl continued on, paying him no mind, "I have experience with such things. You are still so young. Believe me, I know what I speak of. Oh, and by the way, I would never interfere with your family affairs." Again he rolled his eyes musingly, and he was so convinced of his opinion that Bambi held his tongue.

CHAPTER 8

Another night passed, and the morning brought new excitement.

Under a cloudless sky, a morning dawned, fresh and full of dew. All the leaves on the trees and bushes had suddenly begun to smell stronger. The meadow seemed to breath a new fragrance in wide waves, reaching up to the treetops.

"*Peep*," said the titmice as they awoke. But they saw it was still grey and dim, so they said it once and no more. For some time, it stayed quite still. Then from high above, a rough, crackling crow-call sounded through the air. The crows were awake and visiting each other in the treetops. Immediately, the magpie answered, "*Shakerakschak . . . did you think I was still asleep?*" And hundred voices began to call out from here and there, far and near, very softly, "*Peep! Peep! Pew!*" There was tiredness and a shimmer of dawn in their calls.

Suddenly, a blackbird flew up to the top of a fir. All the way up to the very top she flew, to the bough that thrust its fine arm up into the air and she sat high up and looked out far over all the trees, as the drowsy, pale grey sky far away in the east began to glow and come to life. There she began to sing. She was just a tiny dark spot when gazed at from below. Her little black body could have been mistaken for a withered leaf from afar. But her song floated over the forest like a joyous cheer. The forest came alive. The finches sang, the robins and the goldfinch let themselves be heard. With broad clapping and flapping of their wings, the pigeons soared from one place to another. The pheasants' calls pierced the air; it sounded as if their throats were bursting. Soft and strong was the sound of wings, as birds swooped down from the sleeping trees to the ground. They let out many more calls once they had landed on the ground, with their metallic, bursting squawks and soft cooing. High in the air hawks called sharply and joyfully, "*yayaya!*"

The sun had risen.

"*Deeoow-deeeowww!*" the oriole cheered. He flew between the branches, back and forth, and his yellow, round body glinted in the morning light like a buoyant ball of gold in the air.

Bambi entered the meadow from beneath the great oak tree. The meadow sparkled with dew, smelled of grass, of flowers and wet earth, and whispered with a thousand signs of life. There sat Friend Rabbit and he seemed to be pondering something important. A proud pheasant was walking slowly, nipping here and there at the grass and cautiously surveying the area. Its dark blue, bejeweled neck shone in the sun. Just in front of Bambi stood one of the princes, very close. Bambi had never seen him; indeed, he had never seen any of the fathers from so close. The prince was standing amongst the hazel bush, still veiled by some of its branches. Bambi did not move. He hoped the prince would come out completely, and Bambi wondered if he dared speak to him. He wanted to ask his mother and looked around for her. His mother had wandered off and now stood quite far away with Aunt Ena. Gobo and Faline arrived in this moment and came out of the thicket on the meadow. Bambi stood still and thought to himself. If he wanted to go over to his mother and the others now he would have to pass by the prince. He thought that was rather unbecoming. *"Oh well,"* he thought, *"I do not need to ask my mother for permission first. After all, the old prince spoke to me and I did not tell mother about it. Yes, I will address the prince, I will try it. Let the others look over and see me talking to him. I will say, 'Good morning, my prince!' He cannot get angry with me for that. Should he get angry, well I shall run away quickly."* Bambi struggled with his decision, again faltering.

Then the prince stepped out from the hazel bush onto the meadow.

"Now . . ." thought Bambi.

Suddenly, there was a clap of thunder.

Bambi winced and did not know what had happened.

He saw the prince jump high up into the air and with one jump dashed off past Bambi and into the forest.

Bambi looked around earnestly, the thunderclap still roaring inside him. He saw his mother, Aunt Ena, Gobo, and Faline fleeing to the forest, and he saw Friend Rabbit running away, saw the pheasant fleeing. Bambi realized that the whole forest had suddenly fallen silent, so he hastily jumped back into the thicket.

He had only taken a few steps and then there was the prince, laying before him on the ground. Motionless. Bambi was overcome with horror and did not understand what was wrong. The prince lay there; his shoulder was torn open with a large wound, bloody and dead.

"Don't just stand there!" called out someone from behind him. It was his mother, who galloped over at full speed. "Run!!" she called. "Run as fast as you can!" She did not pause, but kept running, and her order pushed Bambi on further and further, until he had no more strength.

"What was that, mother?" he asked. "What *was* that, mother?"

His mother wheezed as she replied, "That . . . was . . . HIM!"

Bambi shuddered, and they ran.

Finally, they all came to a halt, out of breath and weary.

"What did you say? I beg your pardon, but what did you say?" called out a thin voice from above their heads. Bambi looked up and saw Squirrel was running along the branches.

"I chased after you the entire way," he called, "No, no, that is just terrible!"

"Were you there, too?" asked his mother.

"But of course, I was there," answered Squirrel. "I am shaking all over, my every limb." He sat upright and leaned against his beautiful, towering tail and exposing his white chest and pressed both front paws sentimentally to his heart. "I am beside myself."

"I am also quite weak from the scare," said his mother. "It is inconceivable. Not one of us saw a thing."

"Is that so?" Squirrel was upset. "But you are wrong, though. I did see Him!"

"I did, too!" called another voice. It was Magpie; she flew in and sat down on a branch.

"Me, too!" cried out another from even higher. There sat the Jay on an ash tree. Scattered amongst the tops of other trees were a few crows. They shrieked sullenly, "We had seen Him too!"

They all sat all around them and spoke importantly. They were strangely excited, and they seemed full of anger and anxiety.

"*Who?*" Bambi thought. "*Who did they see?*"

"I tried with all my might," said Squirrel, pressing his paws to his heart. "With all my might, I tried to get the prince's attention."

"And I, too," called the Jay. "No matter how much I yelled, he would not listen to me."

"He did not hear me either," the Magpie chimed in. "I must have called out ten times. I was just about to fly closer to him, I thought to myself just then that if he could not hear me, that I should fly over to the hazel bush that he was standing by. From there he could certainly hear me. But it happened in that moment."

"My voice is louder than yours and I warned him as best I could," spoke the Crow with a bitter tone. "But they pay too little attention to us."

"True, too little indeed," agreed Squirrel.

"One does what one can," said Magpie. "We are certainly not at fault that such a misfortune happened."

"Such a handsome prince," exclaimed Squirrel, "and in the prime of his life."

"Bah!" snarled Jay, "If he had not been so proud, if he would have just listened to us!"

"He was certainly not too proud!" disagreed Squirrel.

Magpie added, "Not prouder than any of the other princes."

"So, you mean dumb!" laughed Jay.

"You are one to talk!" called down Crow from above. "You really can't say much about being dumb. The entire forest knows how dumb you are."

"Who, me?" retorted Jay, astonished. "No one here would accuse me of being dumb. Just forgetful, that's all I am, but dumb . . . !"

"As you wish," said Crow honestly. "Come, forget what I have said. What's important is that the prince did not die because he was proud or stupid, but because one cannot escape Him."

"Hah!" snarled Jay. "I don't like such conversations." He flew off.

Crow continued to speak, "He had even outsmarted many of my kin. He kills as He wishes. Nothing can protect us."

"You always have to be on the lookout," added Magpie.

"You surely do," said Crow sadly. "Good bye." Off he flew, and all his relatives joined him.

Bambi looked about. His mother was not there anymore.

"What were they talking about anyways?" Bambi thought. *"I don't understand half of what they were talking about. Who is this 'He' of whom they speak . . . ? Could it be the same 'He' that I saw in the bushes that one time . . . but no, He did not kill me."*

Bambi now thought of the prince who had been laying on the ground in front of him with a bloody, shredded shoulder. So, he was dead now. Bambi kept on walking. The forest sang again with a thousand voices. The sun pierced through the treetops in broad rays; it was bright everywhere; the foliage began to give off a smell in the sun. High in the air, the hawks called, and somewhere nearby a woodpecker laughed out loud, as if nothing had happened. Bambi was not cheered by this; he felt threatened by something dark. He did not understand how the others could be so cheerful and carefree when life was so difficult and so dangerous. In that moment, he was overcome by the desire to go far away, deeper and deeper into the forest. He was now tempted to turn and go to the thickest part of the forest and seek shelter there. Someplace that was surrounded by impenetrable hedges, so that no one could see in—a place far away. He did not want to go back to the meadow again.

Something stirred in the bush nearby. The movement startled Bambi terribly. Then there stood the Old One before him.

Bambi trembled from within. He wanted to run away but he calmed himself and stood there. The Old One looked at him with great, deep eyes. "Were you there, just now?"

"Yes," said Bambi quietly. His heart beat so strong, he felt it all over.

"Where is your mother?" the Old One asked.

Bambi answered, still very quiet, "I do not know . . ."

The Old One still looked at him. "And now you do not call for her?"

Bambi looked into his great, ice-grey face, looked at his majestic crown of the Old One and suddenly felt full of courage. "No, I am not afraid to be alone," he said.

The Old One studied him for a moment, then he spoke softly, "Wasn't it you who not long ago cried for his mother?"

Bambi was a bit ashamed by these words, but he stayed brave. "Yes, that was me," he admitted.

The Old One looked at him in silence, and Bambi felt as if those deep eyes now looked at him a bit softer. "You scolded me then for that, my great Crown Prince," he replied, enraptured, "because I could not be left alone. Since then, I have been able to be alone."

The Old One examined Bambi and smiled, ever so slightly, so that it was hardly noticeable, but Bambi noticed it indeed.

"Please, great Crown Prince," he asked trustfully, "What was it that happened? I don't think I understand it . . . who is this 'He' that everyone speaks of . . . ?" He paused, startled by the dark gaze that now silenced him.

Again, some time passed. The Old One looked beyond Bambi into the distance and then he spoke slowly, "Hear, smell, and see for yourself. Learn for yourself." With that he raised his crowned head even higher. "Farewell," he said nothing more. Then he disappeared.

Bambi stood there, dismayed and confused. He was so discouraged, but the "Farewell" rang in his mind and comforted him. "*Farewell,*" the Old One had said. So, he was not angry.

Bambi felt filled with pride, and he felt solemn seriousness. "Yes," he thought, *life was difficult and full of dangers.* Come what may, he would learn to endure everything.

Slowly, he went deeper into the forest.

CHAPTER 9

The great oak on the edge of the meadow began to lose its leaves. They began to fall from all the trees. One branch on the oak tree stood high above the other branches and leaned out far into the meadow. At the tip of this branch, two leaves still were attached together.

"It is not like it used to be," said one of the leaves.

"No," replied the other. "So many of us fell again last night . . . we are the only leaves left on our branch."

"You never know who will fall," said the first leaf. "Sometimes, back when it was still summer, and the sun warmed us, a storm or a burst of clouds would come and many of us would be torn away, no matter how young we were. You never know who will fall."

"Now the sun does not shine anymore," sighed the second leaf, "And when the sun does come out, it hardly gives us any energy. We need new energy."

"Well that is true, but others will come in our place others when we are gone, and then again others will follow them, and again, and again . . . it is true," the first replied.

"It is certainly true," the second whispered, "It is hard to even imagine such things . . . it is beyond us . . ."

"And how sad it makes me to think of it," added the first.

They were silent for some time. Then the first one spoke quietly once more, thinking aloud, "Why must we all go . . . ?"

The second asked, "What happens to us when we fall off . . . ?"

"We just flutter down . . ."

"What is down there?"

The first answered, "I don't know. Some say this, others say that . . . but nobody knows."

The second asked, "If we feel it, will we still know what happens when we fall down there?"

The first replied, "Who knows? None of the fallen ever came back to tell us of it."

Again, they were both quiet. The first leaf then began to speak tenderly to the other, "Do not think such sad thoughts, it makes me tremble!"

"Alright" answered the second, "Even I am trembling a bit now. Sometimes I don't feel so secure here."

"We should not speak of such things anymore," said the first leaf.

The other retorted, "No . . . we should stop, but . . . what should we speak of then?" It then became silent for some time before continuing, "Which one of us will fall first . . . ?"

"Ah, that will take some time," soothed the first one. "Let's think of how lovely it was, how absolutely lovely it was, when the sun came and heated us up so that our edges got crisp. Do you remember that? Oh, and then the dew in the morning hours . . . and all the lovely, gentle nights . . ."

"Now the nights are terrible," complained the second, "and they seem to go on forever."

"We should not complain," said the first one, mildly. "We have lived much longer than so many others."

"Have I changed very much?" inquired the second leaf shyly, but urgently.

"Not a bit," protested the first, "You don't honestly think that just because *I* have become yellow and ugly . . . No, it is a bit different in my case . . ."

"Oh, come," refuted the second one.

"No, no honestly," repeated the first, full of enthusiasm, "Believe me! You are as beautiful as on your first day. Little yellow stripes here and there, but hardly noticeable, and they just make you more beautiful. Believe me!"

"Thank you," whispered the second leaf, touched by the words. "I don't believe you . . . not entirely . . . but I thank you, because you are so kind, you have always been so kind to me . . . I just now have come to realize how truly kind you were all this time."

"Be still," said the first and fell silent. It could no longer speak as it was overcome with grief.

So, they were both silent. Hours passed. A wet wind blew, cold and menacing, through the treetops.

"Oh . . . now . . ." said the second leaf, ". . . I . . ." Its voice cracked. It was gently released from its place on the branch and floated down. And thus, winter began.

CHAPTER 10

Bambi realized that the world had changed. It was hard for him to get used to going out into this transformed world. They had all lived decadent, rich lives, and now they lived a kind of poverty. But Bambi only knew the wealth. He had taken it for granted to be surrounded by the greatest abundance of the finest luxuries: to have no worries about food; to sleep in the beautiful green den where no one could look in; and to walk in a splendidly smooth, shimmering red coat.

Now everything had changed slowly, without him actually noticing it. To him, the process of change was just a series of amusing new events and appearances. It entertained him to watch the milk-white fogs of mist clear from the meadow in the morning, or when a fog suddenly sank down from the early twilight sky and then disappeared so beautifully in the sun. He also liked the frost that spread across the soil on the meadow, leaving it white. For a while he rejoiced to hear his great relatives, the deer, calling out to each other. The whole forest vibrated with the voices of the kings. Bambi listened and was very afraid, but his heart quivered with admiration at the sound of these great thundering calls. He thought of the great crowns that the kings wore, as big and complex as strong tree branches, and he thought their voice was as mighty as their crowns. When he heard the powerful outburst of such a call, then he stopped and stood still. A commanding urge flowed through the deep sounds, the tremendous moans of these proud creatures that had become furious, and a primitive force surged from within—longing, anger, and pride. Bambi fought in vain against his fear. It overwhelmed him to hear these voices, but he was proud to be of such a distinguished species. At the same time, he felt a strangely bothered that they were so distant. It hurt and humiliated him, not that he exactly understood why or how—more so that he was aware of it.

Bambi discovered he had many new interests once the mating season of the kings was over and their thunderous voices were quieted. Then, when he wandered the forest at night or spent the day laying in his den, he could hear the whisper of leaves falling from the trees. The air ceaselessly crinkled and crackled all of the treetops, every branch. There was a steady flow of a gentle silver hue falling to the earth. It was wonderful to watch, and it was delicious to fall asleep to the sounds of this secretive, wistful whispering. Soon there were piles of loose leaves stacked high on the ground, and when he walked about it made a loud noise, murmuring loudly and rustling softly. It was a funny feeling to have to push aside so many leaves with each step—that was how high the piles now lay. It made a *tsiscsh-tsiscsh*—so fine, so light and silver. It was quite practical, too, as in these days he hardly needed to listen or sense with much effort in order to know what was happening nearby. One could easily hear everything from far away. The smallest movement caused a crinkle or yelled out *tsiscsh!* Who could sneak up on you? No one.

Then came the rain. It came down in streams from the early morning to the late evening, then clapping and splashing from late evening, all night until the next morning, then stopping for a while only to start again with the same power as it began before. The air seemed to be filled with cold water—the entire world seemed full of it. Just eating a few blades of grass would fill one's mouth with water, and simply tugging at a single straw would bring a cascade of water down onto your eyes or nose. The leaves did not make their noises anymore. They all just lay there, wet and heavy, on the ground, flatted from the rain and making not a sound. Bambi witnessed for the first time what it was like to be soaked for days and nights by pouring rain—rain that could reach down through his thick coat to his skin. He did not freeze, but he longed for the warmth, and he thought it was a wretched thing to have to walk around soaked to the bone.

But Bambi came to understand what freezing cold was when the north storm came. It didn't even help to cuddle up to his mother anymore. Yes, of course, he thought it was a lovely thing at first, to snuggle so close and to at least have one side kept warm. But the winds whirled throughout the forest all day and all night. It seemed as if he were driven to the point of madness by an incomprehensible, icy-cold anger, and it was as if he wanted to tear the forest up from all its roots and carry it away or destroy it. The trees fought against the mighty wind; they fought tremendously against its attack. He could hear the trees moaning, sighing, creaking, and sometimes the loud bang of strong branches being split, the angry crash with which the trunk of a tree broke, and the defeated tree then crying out from all the wounds of his divided and dying body. Then there was nothing else to be heard, because the grim storm grew even stronger over the forest and was so loud that its roar devoured all the other voices.

Now Bambi understood that hard times had come. He saw how the rain and storm had changed the world. There was not a single leaf left on a tree or bush. They all stood naked, as if every leaf had been stolen and they stretched their naked brown arms pitifully to the sky. The grass on the meadow had withered and was now blackish-brown and so short that it looked as if it were burned down to just above the earth. Even in his den it was now so empty and bleak. Since the green walls had disappeared, it was now so hard to find privacy like before and the cold crept in from all sides.

One day, a young magpie flew across the meadow. Something white and cold fell in its eye, again and again, and it formed a veil that blocked her view. Small, soft, brilliant white flakes danced around her. The magpie flapped her wings hard, pointed herself upwards, and climbed higher in the air, all in vain. The white, cold flakes were still there and still fell in her eyes. So once more she pointed her beak up in the air and climbed even higher.

"Don't even try, my dear creature," a crow that was flying over her in the same direction called down to her. "Just don't even work so hard. You cannot fly high enough to get out of these flakes. That is snow."

"Snow?" The magpie was astonished and fought against the snowstorm.

"Well yes," said the crow, "It's winter, you see. That is snow."

"Pardon me," retorted the magpie, "I just left the nest this May. I don't know of this winter."

"Oh, that happens to many," remarked the crow. "You will get to know it soon enough."

"Well, if this is snow," said the magpie, "then I will just sit down for a bit." She landed on an alder branch and shook the snow off.

The crow continued to fly slowly onwards.

At first, Bambi was excited about the snow. The air was quiet and mild as the white stars floated down, and then the world looked like new. Bambi thought it was brighter, even more joyous, and if the sun came out, even for a short time, then the blanket of white lit up, flashing and glowing so mightily that it could blind you.

Soon Bambi stopped getting excited about the snow. It made it much harder to find food. First, he had to scrape away the snow and it took so much energy just to find a small withered piece of grass. Also, the frozen snow scraped at his legs and one had to be careful not to get any wounds. Gobo already had some. Of course, Gobo was not very tough and his mother often worried about him.

Now they almost always spent their time together and felt much closer to each other than earlier. Aunt Ena always came with her children. Recently, Marena, an almost full-grown young girl, came too. Old Ms. Nettla did most of the talking when they were together. She was alone but had her thoughts to keep her company. "No," she said, "I don't bother myself with children anymore. I have had enough of that fun."

Faline dared ask, "Why so? If it is so fun?" and then Ms. Nettla acted as if she was angry and said, "It is not a good kind of fun and I've had enough of that."

Everyone enjoyed the conversations. They all sat together and chatted. The children never had as much to listen to as in the winter. Even the princes joined them from time to time. At the beginning it was a bit strange, especially because the children were so shy. But even that changed and everything became quite relaxed. Bambi was in awe of Ronno, who was a strong buck, and the young, handsome Karus was his favorite. They had both shed their crowns and Bambi often stared in amazement at the slate-grey, round, flat spots on the heads of the princes; they sparkled and had many soft nubs. How noble they looked.

It was quite exciting when a prince had a story to tell. Ronno had a very large, fur-covered lump on his front left leg. He would not step on this leg with all his weight and sometimes he asked, "Can you tell that I limp?" Then everyone would quickly disagree, saying that it was hardly noticeable. That was what Ronno wanted to hear. Though in all honesty, it was not very noticeable.

"Yes," he then would continue, "I just barely made it out of a bad situation that time." Then Ronno would tell the story of the of that time. But he had only injured his leg a bit, back then. It hurt enough to be bothersome. No wonder. The bone had shattered, but Ronno kept calm. He had to flee on just three legs. On and on, no matter how tired he was, he kept running for he knew he was being chased after. He ran and ran until night fell. Then he let himself rest. But the next morning, he continued to run far away until he felt safe. Eventually he stopped and cared for his wound, but he stayed alone and hid, waiting for the wound to close. Finally, when it had healed, he went back to the deer and was a hero. Now he limped, but it was hardly noticeable.

Now that everyone spent so much time together in the cold and many stories were told, Bambi heard about Him more than before. They talked about how horrible He was. Nobody could bear to look into His pale face—Bambi remembered from seeing Him. They also spoke of the scent that He brought with Him, and Bambi could have spoken up about this too, but he knew better than to get involved in the conversations of the grown-ups. They said that the scent had mysterious way of changing a thousand times and yet it was always recognizable, because it was always strangely exciting, mystifying, mysterious, and at times, horrible. They said He only walked on two legs and they told of the wonderful power of His two hands. A few did not know exactly what that was, *hands*. Someone explained it.

Then Ms. Nettla exclaimed, "I don't think it is really remarkable. Squirrel can do all those things, just like every little mouse can do the same." She turned her head away disdainfully. "Uh-uh!" called out some of the others in disagreement; it clearly was not the same as what He could do.

But Ms. Nettla was not convinced otherwise, "And what of the hawk? And the buzzard? And the owl? They all just have two legs and if they want to carry something, as you all call it, then they just simply stand on one leg and carry it with the other leg. That is much more difficult, and He can certainly not do that." Ms. Nettla admired nothing about Him. She hated Him with all her heart. "He is disgusting," she said and left it at that. No one disagreed with her, for no one liked Him. But the matter became more complicated when it was said that He had a third hand—not just two hands, but a third.

"That's an old tale," declared Ms. Nettla, "I do not believe it."

"So?" Ronno interrupted, "And how did He injure my leg? What do you say about that?"

Ms. Nettla answered carelessly, "That's your business, my dear, I am not the one who broke something—"

Aunt Ena chimed in, "I've seen Him a lot in my life, and I think it is a bit too much to say that He has a third hand."

The young Karus politely remarked, "I agree with you on that. I am friends with a crow . . ." He paused for a moment and looked at each one in turn, as if he feared being laughed at. When he saw that everyone was listening attentively, he continued, "This crow is quite smart, I must say that, she is amazingly educated . . . and she said that He really has three hands, but not always. The third hand, so says the crow, is the evil one. It did not grow like the other two, but it hangs over

His shoulder. The crow says she knows exactly if He—or any of His kin—is dangerous or not. If He comes without the third hand, then He is not dangerous."

Ms. Nettla laughed, "Your crow is a dumb creature, my dear Karus, you tell her I said so. If she is as smart as she thinks, then she would know that He is always dangerous, always—" But the others objected.

Bambi's mother said, "There are some of them who are not dangerous at all. You can tell immediately."

"So?" Asked Mrs. Nettla, "What, do you just stand there until they come up and say hello to them?"

Bambi's mother replied softly, "Of course I do not stop, I run away."

Faline blurted out, "You must always run away!" Everyone laughed. But when they continued to talk about the third hand, they became serious, and gradually fear crept in. For whatever it was—a third hand or something else—it was awful, and they did not understand it. Most of them only knew of it from the stories of others, but some of them had seen it for themselves: He stood there, far away, and did not move. One could not explain what he was doing, nor how it happened, but suddenly there was a clap of thunder, fire spurted, and far away from him one collapsed with a torn chest, only to die. They all crouched as they spoke of this, feeling as if a dark force was hanging over them. They eagerly listened to the many stories, full of terrors—of blood and woe. Taking in everything that was said. Even stories that were certainly made up, all the tales and legends that came from the grandfathers and great-grandfathers, and in every story, they searched without knowing it, for a way to reconcile this dark force, or how to escape it.

"So, what do we do?" asked the young Karus wearily. "How is it that He can stand so far away and still harm us?"

"What does your clever crow say about it, no explanation?" sneered Ms. Nettla.

"No," smiled Karus, "She did say, though, that she has often seen this and still cannot explain it. No one can."

"Well, He can knock the crows down out of a tree if he wants to," commented Ronno.

"And He can bring a pheasant down out of the sky," added Aunt Ena.

Bambi's mother said, "He throws his hand. My grand-mother told me that."

"Well then," asked Ms. Nettla, "and what is it that makes that terrible thundering?"

"Well, when He throws His hand," explained Bambi's mother, "that is when the fire flashes; it rumbles like thunder. He must have fire inside of him."

"Pardon me," Ronno spoke, "That He is made out of fire is correct. But this about His hand, nonsense. A hand could not make such wounds. You will see for yourself. It is more like a tooth that He throws after us. Look, a tooth explains a lot. And you can die from a bite."

Young Karus sighed deeply, "Will He ever stop chasing us?"

Now it was Marena, the girl who was almost grown up, who spoke, "It is said that one day, He will come to us and be as gentle as we are. He will play with us and the entire forest will be joyous and live in harmony."

Ms. Nettla burst out laughing, "He should stay where He is and leave us alone!"

Aunt Ena gently added, "We must not say such things."

"Why ever not?" countered Ms. Nettla hotly. "I must dis-agree. Live in harmony! As long as we can remember, He kills us, all of us—our sisters, our mothers, our brothers! As long as we have been on this earth, He leaves us no peace. He kills us wherever we roam . . . and then you say we should forgive Him and make peace with Him? What nonsense!"

Marena looked at everyone with her big eyes that shone calmly. "Forgiveness is not nonsense," she spoke. "We should all hope for forgiveness."

Ms. Nettla turned away. "I am going to find something to eat," she said and left.

CHAPTER 11

Winter continued on. Sometimes it was milder, but then snow would fall and pile up higher and higher, so that it was almost impossible to scrape it away. The worst was when it thawed and the snow that melted to water would then freeze overnight. This created a thin layer of ice that was very slippery. The ice would break often, and its sharp splinters would cut into the tender skin on the deer's legs. Now there had been a deep frost for days. The air was clear and thin as never before, and full of energy. It began to ring in a fine, high tone. It sang from the cold.

The woods were silent, but every day something terrible happened. Once the crows attacked the young son of the rabbits, who was sick anyway, and cruelly killed him. His pain echoed for a long time. Friend Rabbit was out in the forest when he received the sad news; he could not believe it. Another time, a squirrel suffered a large wound—it was bit by a weasel on the throat. Miraculously, the squirrel had managed to escape. It could not speak from the pain, but ran through all the branches. Everyone could see it. From time to time it paused, sat down, desperately lifted its front paws, and clutched its head in its terror and grief, as the red blood rushed down its white chest. It ran around for an hour, then it suddenly collapsed, hit the branches clumsily, and fell dying into the snow. Immediately, a few magpies came in to start their feast. Another time, the fox caught the beautiful, strong pheasant, which had been so loved and respected. His death caused great sadness throughout the forest and the poor widow could not be consoled. The fox had pulled the pheasant out of its hiding place in the snow, where it had believed itself to be well hidden. No one felt safe anymore after this happened—in the middle of the day, nonetheless. There was a sense of great alarm that seemed to never end, and everyone grew bitter and rude. Everything changed: no one behaved with good manners, and the animals showed each other no kindness. It destroyed confidence. There was no mercy, no rest, no restraint.

"One can hardly imagine that it will get better again," sighed Bambi's mother.

Aunt Ena sighed, too. "One can hardly remember that it was used to be different."

"Oh, that's not so," said Marena and looked about, "I think of it quite often, how lovely it used to be!"

"I say," Ms. Nettla said, speaking to Aunt Ena, "Your son is shivering so!" She nodded to Gobo. "Does he always shiver like that?"

"Sadly, yes," answered Aunt Ena, worry in her voice. "He has for many days now."

"Well," said Ms. Nettla in very direct manner, "I am just glad that I don't have children anymore. If that were my child, I would be worried he would not live through the winter."

Gobo really did not look well. He was weak, as he had always been more delicate than Bambi or Faline, and had never grown quite as big as the others. Now, however, he seemed to be weaker each day. He could hardly eat the food that there was. Eating it would cause him such pain. He had no energy from all the cold and nausea. He always trembled and could barely stand. Everyone looked after him.

Ms. Nettla walked over to him and playfully nudged his side with her nose, "Now come, don't be sad," said firmly, "It is unbecoming for a young prince, and it's not good for you." She turned away, so that no one could see how touched with sadness she was.

Ronno, who had just been looking for food in the snow, a bit further off, leapt up. "I don't know what that was . . ." he whispered and looked about.

Everyone now paid attention. "What was . . . what?" they all asked.

"I don't know," repeated Ronno, "but something isn't right . . . suddenly, I feel restless, as if . . . something is going on . . ."

Karus checked the air. "I don't sense anything strange," he declared.

They all stood about, sensing the air and listening carefully. "Nothing!"

"Nothing to see . . ." they all said, one after another.

"Still!" Ronno insisted, "You can think what you want, but . . . something is wrong . . ."

Marena said, "The crows called . . ."

"Listen, they are calling again!" Faline said hastily, but by now the others had heard it, too.

"They are flying away!" pointed out Karus.

Everyone looked up. High above the treetops, the crows flew in their direction. They were coming from the edge of the forest, over where the danger always came from and they called out gloomily to each other. Something out of the ordinary had startled them.

"You see, I was right." spoke Ronno. "Something is wrong!"

should we do?" whispered Bambi's mother, quite

away, now!" said Aunt Ena nervously

"No, wait!" commanded Ronno.

"Wait? With the children?" Aunt Ena disagreed. "Gobo cannot even walk!"

"Well fine," Ronno said. "Leave with the children, but I don't think it is a good idea and I have said so now." He was stern and direct.

"Come, Gobo! Faline, come! Quietly! Slowly! Follow me," warned Aunt Ena.

She snuck off with the children. Some time passed. They stood still, listening and sensing for something in the air.

"This is just what we need now," began Ms. Nettla, "To endure this now!" She was very angry. Bambi looked and her and felt that she was thinking something terrible.

Now came the magpies from the same part of the thicket where the crows had just flown from. Three, four all at once. "Beware! Beware, beware, beware!" they cried. They were not visible, but their echoing call became mumbled as they called out over each other, cautioning, "Beware, beware, beware!" Suddenly, they were above the deer; they fluttered on, restless and startled.

"*Ca-caw!*" cried Jay, sounding the alarm.

Suddenly, all of the deer stood close together. As if there had been something that pressed them from all sides. They stood still and inhaled.

It was Him.

A wave of smells flooded from Him, more intense than ever. There was no need to sniff at the air, His scent forced its way into their noses, fogging their senses and freezing their hearts.

The magpies still shuddered, Jay rattled overhead, everything was alive and calling out. The titmice peeped from the branches, hundreds of small feathered balls chirping, "Away! Away!" A blackbird darted through the trees—a lightning-fast streak of black with a prolonged chirping cry. The deer peered out through the dark woven fence of the bare branches; all they saw against the white snowy ground were narrow, little shadowy shapes that darted confusedly about, back and forth. It was the pheasants. Something shimmered red in a corner. It was a fox. This time nobody was afraid of him, for there came a constant wave of this terrible smell that breathed horror into their hearts and brought them all together, for they shared one great fear, and one great desire to flee, to save themselves.

This mysterious and overwhelming smell pierced the forest with such power that they all recognized he could not be alone, but that he came with more of his kind and they were there for one thing. No one moved, they looked at the titmice who scurried away with rapid flutters, the blackbirds, the squirrels who jumped in racing leaps from treetop to treetop, and they thought that all these small creatures need not fear this danger, but still they fled when they felt His presence. For no creature of the forest could stand Him being there.

Now Friend Rabbit hopped slowly over, sat still, then hopped on.

"What is it?" Karus called out impatiently after him.

But Friend Rabbit only looked about with wild eyes and could not speak. He was terribly distressed.

"Why even ask . . . ?" said Ronno darkly.

Friend Rabbit gasped for breath. "We are surrounded," he said flatly. "There is no way out. He is everywhere!"

At that moment, they heard His voice. Twenty or thirty times He cried out, "*Hoho! Haha!*" It was more shocking than a thunderstorm. He beat on the trunks of the tree; it sounded like drumming. How terrifying it was. Distant noises and the

ɔf splitting bushes could be heard, along with shrieks
ʃrashing of broken branches.

ɔpeared!—He appeared there in the thicket.

A whistling, a short trilling, and the rustle of unfolding
wings sounded behind Him. It was a pheasant, taking off
from close by. They heard the pheasant's wings beating, the
sound grew quieter as he flew higher into the air. Then a
brilliant clap of thunder. Silence. Then a dull thud on the
ground.

"The pheasant has fallen," Bambi's mother's voice quaked.

"The first . . ." added Ronno.

Marena said, "In this hour, some of us will die. Maybe I
will be one of them." No one listened to her now that the
great danger was there.

Bambi tried to think, but the raging sounds that now
swelled higher and higher tore every thought apart. Bambi
could only hear these sounds. They were deafening and amidst
all the growls, crackling, and crying, he could hear his own
heartbeat pounding. He felt strange and did not know why
his limbs trembled so. Now and again his mother spoke into
his ear, "Just stay close to me." She yelled it, but in the din it
sounded as if she was whispering. It gave him strength. It held
him there where he stood, like a chain, or else he would have
wildly run away. He heard her voice again, each time when
he was just about to run in panic.

He looked around. The forest was swarming with all kinds
of blindly confused animals. A few weasels ran past—thin,
scampering stripes that he was barely able to track. A polecat
listened intently to everything Friend Rabbit could report.
There the fox stood in a jumble of fleeing pheasants. They did
not pay attention to him; they ran right under his nose and he
did not even bother to try and catch them. He stood alert, with
pointed ears and twitching nose, listening to the approaching

tumult. Only his tail moved, softly whipping back and forth. He was vigilant. A pheasant hurried by, trembling in fear—he was beside himself. "Don't take off!!" he called to the other pheasants. "Don't take off . . . just run! Don't fly off! No one take off! Just run, run, run!" He repeated himself again and again as if he was reminding himself. He didn't know what he was saying. "*Hoho! Haha!*" It seemed the danger was getting closer. "Do not take off!" called the pheasant once more. Yet in the same moment, a wheezing sob broke his voice and with a great rustle, he spread his wings and took off. Bambi watched him; he climbed straight and steep, up through the trees. His flapping wings were splendid, shimmering with metallic dark blues, and the golden-brown shine of his body as magnificent as jewels. The drag of his long tail feathers swept proudly behind him. A short, sharp clap of thunder. The pheasant twitched mid-air, turned his head back as if he was grabbing at his leg with his beak, and fell to the ground with a mighty crash. He fell amidst the others on the ground and did not move.

Chaos broke out. Everyone ran about, stumbling over each other. Five or six pheasants tried to take off with a loud clamor. "Don't fly away," called the others as they ran off. Again, the thunder clapped five, then six times. Those that had tried to fly away fell to the ground with a lifeless thud.

"Come on!" said Bambi's mother. Bambi looked about. Ronno and Karus were already gone. Ms. Nettla fled. Only Marena was still there. Bambi went with his mother and Marena followed timidly. Such chaos rang out around them—wild crashes, roars, thunderclaps all around them. His mother was composed. She trembled ever so slightly, but she kept calm. "Bambi, my child," she said, "stay behind me no matter what. We have to make it out of here and through the clearing. Now we must go slowly."

The roaring became louder and more frequent. Ten, eleven, twelve times, He threw thunder with His hands.

"Come on, further," said his mother. "Do not run! Not until we have to go through the clearing, then we must run as fast as we can. Do not forget, Bambi, do not look out for me when we are out there. Even if I should fall, do not turn . . . just go, keep going farther and farther! Do you understand, Bambi?"

His mother went slowly in spite of all the noise, carefully, one step at a time. The pheasants ran like wild, hiding in the snow, fleeing, trying to take to the air. The entire family of rabbits hopped about, sometimes standing still, then hopping again frantically. No one said a word. They were all exhausted from the anxiety, paralyzed by the roaring noises and thunder claps.

It grew brighter ahead of Bambi and his mother. The clearing glinted through the bushes. Behind them, the crunching and snapping of twigs grew closer, the drumming noises were louder now, and it bellowed again, *"Haha"* and *"Hoho!"*

Nearby, Friend Rabbit and two of his cousins ran out into the clearing. *Bam! Bang, bam!* The thunder clapped again. Bambi saw Friend Rabbit turn a somersault as he ran, his pale belly turned upwards and then stayed that way. He trembled and then was still. Bambi was petrified.

Behind him someone called out, "They are here! Everyone get out!"

A hasty jumble of whistling, flapping wings, anxious fluttering, and many wild calls ensued. The pheasants all took off together. Thunder pierced the air again, and the firm thuds of the fallen could be heard, mixed with the faint whistling of those who escaped.

Bambi heard footsteps and looked back. There He was. He came out from between the bushes, here and there, again and again. He showed up everywhere, trampling about, shredding the growth, drumming against the trunks of trees, and screaming in that terrible voice.

"NOW!" said his mother. "Straight away! Keep some distance!" And just like that she was off, kicking up a dust of snow. Bambi raced out into it after her. Thunder claps came from every direction. It was as if the earth was being torn in two. Bambi saw nothing, he ran. He only wanted to flee from this chaos, away from the haze and confusion of these smells, he could only feel the need to flee. He was overcome by the need to save himself. He ran. He thought for a moment that he saw his mother fall, but he was not sure, how could he know? There was a veil of fear around him; it erupted from within him as the thunder roared around him. He could do nothing, think of nothing, he just ran.

After he had crossed the opening, he entered the safety of a different thicket. Behind him there was another sharp clap of thunder and a scream rang out, and in the branches above him, there was a short spray of pebbles. Then it was quieter for a moment. Bambi ran on. A dying pheasant lay there with a twisted neck and it weakly beat its wings against the snow. As the pheasant heard Bambi coming, it stopped moving and whispered, "It is over . . ."

Bambi paid him no mind and ran onward. A jumble of bushes blocked his way, forcing him to look for a new path. He stamped about on the ground, impatiently.

"Here, over here," called someone with a weak voice. Bambi instinctively walked towards it and it lead him to a passable trail. Ahead on the trail, someone stood up before him. It was the Rabbit's wife. She had called out to him. "Would you please help me?" she said. Bambi looked at her and was shocked. Her hind legs dragged lifelessly in the snow, which melted, stained red by the hot blood. Once again, she said, "Would you please help me?" She spoke as if she had been sent by someone, calm and almost cheerful. "I do not know what happened to me," she continued, "but, it certainly does not matter . . . but, right now . . . I just cannot walk right now . . ." In the middle of her sentence, she sank to one side and was dead. Bambi was again seized with horror and ran.

"Bambi?"

He came to a halt. He knew the voice, it was one of his kind.

Again, it asked "Bambi . . . Is that you?"

There was Gobo, helpless, stuck in the snow. He had no energy, he could hardly stand up; he just lay there, too weak to do more than raise his head. Bambi ran to his side.

"Where is your mother, Gobo?" he asked, gasping for air. "And where is Faline?" Bambi spoke quickly, anxious and impatient. His heart still throbbed with nervousness.

"My mother and Faline had to go," answered Gobo. He spoke quietly, but as aware and serious as an adult. "They had to leave me here. I fell. You must go, too, Bambi."

"Up!" yelled Bambi. "Stand up, Gobo! You have had time to rest, now stand up. Come now, up. Come with me!"

"No, let me be," rejected Gobo, "I cannot get up now. It is not possible. I want to, so badly, Bambi, you can imagine, but I am too weak."

"What if something happens to you?" demanded Bambi.

"Well I don't know, I imagine I will die," said Gobo simply.

Again, noises came from behind them and ringing out above. The thunder had come, too. Bambi startled. He heard branches nearby, cracking, something was there. Then out of the forest galloped the young Karus, quickening through the snow towards them. "Run!" he called, having seen Bambi. "Don't just stand there, if you can, run!" In no time, he had passed, and his wild retreat carried Bambi off. He hardly noticed that he had started to run again and then after a moment, he called back "Farewell, Gobo." But he was too far gone. Gobo could not hear him anymore.

He ran in the forest which was engulfed by the noise and thunder. It lasted until evening. When darkness fell, it became calm. A light breeze soon blew away the heinous scent that was everywhere. But the fear remained. The first familiar face Bambi saw was Ronno. Now he limped more than before. "There beneath the oak tree," said Ronno, "is the fox, he has fever from his wounds. I just went by there. It is terrible how he suffers. He is mad."

"Have you seen my mother?" asked Bambi.

"No," answered Ronno shyly and quickly disappeared.

Later that night, Bambi found Ms. Nettla with Faline. They were all overjoyed to see each other.

"Have you seen my mother?" asked Bambi.

"No," answered Faline. "I don't even know where my mother is."

"My," said Ms. Nettla merrily, "what a lovely present. I was happy that I did not have my own children to look after and now I have two at once to look after! Oh, thank you!"

Bambi and Faline laughed.

They spoke of Gobo. Bambi said that he had found him, and they began to cry. But Ms. Nettla did not allow them to cry. "Now we have to try and find something to eat. It is unbelievable. The entire day without a bite to eat." She led them both to a place where there was still a bit of low hanging foliage. Ms. Nettla was very wise. She ate nothing herself but encouraged Bambi and Faline to eat well. She found a grassy place and said; "Here . . . that's good," or she said, "No, wait . . . we'll find something better." Now and again she scolded, "How foolish! You children are such trouble!"

Suddenly, they saw Aunt Ena and ran towards her "Aunt Ena!" called Bambi. He had seen her first. Faline was overjoyed and jumped high into the air. "Mother!"

But Ena cried and was weak. "Gobo is gone," she said. "I

searched for him; I was at his bed, back in the snow where he had fallen . . . everywhere . . . they were empty. He is gone . . . my poor, dear Gobo . . ."

Ms. Nettla grumbled, "If you would have just looked for a sign of him, tracks, that would have been smarter than crying."

"There were no tracks," said Aunt Ena.

"But, he . . . he left many tracks. I came across Gobo . . ."

Everyone was silent. Then Bambi asked, discouraged, "Aunt Ena . . . you didn't see my mother, did you?"

"No," answered Aunt Ena quietly.

Bambi never saw his mother again.

CHAPTER 12

The pussy willows had lost their buds long ago and now everything began to turn green. The young leaves on the bushes and trees were still very small. The soft glimmer of these early mornings made them look like little children that have just awakened from sleep.

Bambi stood before a hazel bush and rubbed his antlers against the bark. How lovely it felt. It was necessary that he do this. The velvety fur that wrapped his antlers must come off, naturally, and no one ever waited for this to fall off on its own. Bambi rubbed the antlers again so that the velvet would loosen and entire strips of it would fall and dangle next to his ears. As he rubbed against the hazel bush, he felt his crown of antlers was harder than the branches of the hazel This filled him with a sensation of pride and strength. He then used more effort and ripped longer felt pieces off of his crown. The bare white of the wood appeared, and no sooner was the wood exposed, it began to turn rust-red. Bambi paid no attention to it. He saw the light, inner wood becoming more exposed with each stroke and it amused him. There were other hazel bushes or dogwood branches around him that showed signs of his hard work.

"Well, it looks like you are almost done . . ." said a voice from behind him.

Bambi turned his head about and looked around.

There sat Squirrel, looking kindly at him.

Bambi and Squirrel were both startled by a sound. A woodpecker that sat on the branch of the oak tree called down, "Excuse me . . . I just can't help but laugh when I see you in such a state."

"What's there to laugh about?" asked Bambi politely.

"Well," stated the woodpecker, "You're going about it all wrong. First of all, you need to pick the stronger trees, you won't get anything out of the hazel bush."

"What do you mean, I won't get anything out of it, what should I get?" inquired Bambi.

"Beetles . . ." laughed the woodpecker. "Beetles and larvae . . . You see, this is how you have to do it!" He drummed on the trunk of the oak. *Tok, tok, tok, tok.*

Squirrel rushed up to him and scolded, "What are you talking about? The Prince is not looking for beetles and larvae . . ."

"Why not?" said the woodpecker jovially. "They taste delicious . . ." He pecked at one of the beetles he had found, swallowed it, and went back to drumming.

"You don't understand, do you?" the Squirrel continued to scold, "Such a noble sire has different purposes than you . . . you are just embarrassing yourself . . ."

"That's no bother to me," answered the woodpecker. "I have my own higher purposes," he called out and fluttered away.

Squirrel scurried down the tree.

"Don't you remember me?" he asked and made a friendly face.

"I believe I do," answered Bambi kindly, "You live up there, don't you?" he leaned his head back to point up the oak tree.

The squirrel looked at him merrily. "You have me confused with my grandmother," he said, "Yes, I thought you had me confused with my grandmother. My grandmother used to live up there when you were just a child, Prince Bambi. She told me many stories about you. Yes . . . but then she was killed by a weasel . . . a long time ago, in the winter . . . don't you remember?"

"Of course." Bambi nodded. "I heard about it."

"Anyways . . . and after that my father moved in," explained the squirrel. He perched upright, widened his eyes, and held both of his front paws gently on his white chest. "But . . . maybe you had me confused with my father . . . Did you know my father?"

"I'm sorry," replied Bambi, "I never had the pleasure of meeting him."

"Oh, I thought so!" called Squirrel happily. "My father was so grumpy and shy. He never had much to do with others."

"Where is he now?" inquired Bambi.

"Ah," said the squirrel, "He was caught by an owl a month ago. Yes, so now I live here. I am quite happy here. You must know that I was born up here, too."

Bambi turned to go.

"Wait!" the squirrel called out quickly, "I didn't come to tell you all this. I wanted to tell you something quite different."

Bambi stood still. "What was it, then?" he asked patiently.

"Yes . . . what was it?" the squirrel thought for a bit, jumped abruptly, composed himself again, and then leaned back on his magnificent tail, looked at Bambi, and said, "Right. Now I've got it. I wanted to say that you are almost done with your crown and that it will be quite lovely."

"Oh, do you think so?" Bambi was elated.

"Quite lovely, indeed!" called the squirrel and pressed its front paws together against its white chest in excitement. "So tall! So regal! And such long, bright points! How rare indeed!"

"Really?" asked Bambi. He was so joyous that he started rubbing again at the hazel bush. Long strips of the bark tumbled down.

Meanwhile the squirrel continued to speak. "I do say, the others of your age don't have such splendid crowns. It seems almost impossible. If someone had known you last summer . . . I saw you a few times, from far away, but one would truly not believe that it was you . . . with those thin little sticks that you had back then . . ."

Bambi stopped short, shocked. "Farewell," he said hastily, "I must continue on!" and he ran off.

He did not like to be reminded of the previous summer. It had been a very difficult time for him. First, his mother had disappeared, and he had felt so alone. The winter had lasted so long back then, and spring did not come in a hurry, it started to turn green so late. Without Ms. Nettla, Bambi would have never survived, but she had taken him in and helped as she could. Still, he was often alone. He missed Gobo the most—poor Gobo, who had probably died like all the others. Bambi often thought of him during this hard time, and he only then realized how loving and kind Gobo had been. He hardly ever saw Faline. She kept close to her mother and was strangely shy.

Later on, when it finally grew warm again, Bambi started to recover. His first crown began to grow, and he was very proud of it. But bitter disappointment soon followed. The other ones who had grown crowns now chased him when they saw him. They charged at him angrily, did not allow anyone else to come close to him; they would fight him and at last, since he was afraid of them chasing him, he would begin to hide himself, wandering along hidden paths. And yet, the hotter and sunnier the days were, more restless he would become. He felt a longing that was painful and comforting at the same time. When he happened to meet Faline or one of her friends from afar, a rush of incomprehensible excitement overcame him. Oftentimes he would just catch a scent of her trail, or he could smell on the breath he drew in that she was near. Each time, he felt irresistibly drawn to them. Should he give in to his longing and go after the scent, it always ended with his misfortune. For either he met no one—and after some time, tired and defeated, he would admit to himself that he was being avoided by the others—or he crossed paths with another crowned deer, one who would strike at him, bucking and chasing him off in disgrace. Ronno and Karus behaved the worst towards him. What an unpleasant time it was.

Now the squirrel had carelessly reminded him of this time. Suddenly, he felt wild and began to run. Birds fluttered out of the bushes where he passed, "Who is that . . . ? Who was that?" Bambi did not hear them. A few magpies nervously shrieked, "Did something happen?" The Jay yelled maliciously, "What has happened?" Bambi ignored him. Above him, the oriole sang in the trees, "Good morning . . . I am so-oh gla-a-d!" Bambi did not respond. The thicket around him was now glowing light from the fine rays of the sun. Bambi did not care. Suddenly, something stirred loudly beneath his feet. A whole rainbow of beautiful colors flashed and shone right before his eyes, and he stopped, blinded. It was Janello, the pheasant, who was startled by Bambi almost trampling him. Scoldingly, he flapped his wings. "Unbelievable!" he yelled with his cracking, screeching voice. Bambi stood perplexed and looked at him. "My, that was close! You just missed me, but how thoughtless . . ." chirped a soft voice next to him on the ground. It was Janelline, the wife of the pheasant. She sat on the ground and brooded. "My husband was terribly frightened," she went on, clearly upset, "and so was I. But I'm not allowed to move from the spot . . . I'm not moving from the spot, no matter what happens . . . you could have crushed me . . ."

Bambi was a bit ashamed, "I beg your pardon," he stuttered. "I was not paying attention."

Janelline answered, "Oh, come! It was not so bad. It's just that my husband and I, we are so nervous right now. You understand . . ."

Bambi did not understand and continued on, but now he was calmer. The forest sang about him. The light turned warmer and golden; the leaves on the branches, the grass on the ground, and the moist earth began to give off their scents. A strong energy began to swell within Bambi and reached out through all his limbs. He began to stir with hesitant and restrained movements that were very stiff, as if he were not real.

He came upon a low elder bush and raised his knees to strike the ground in massive blows. His sharp hooves slashed the grass, the wild peas, and leeks, violets, and snowbells, pawing away at them until the earth before him was bare and dotted with torn plants.

Two moles who had burrowed below an old, wild privet heard the racket and looked over. They observed Bambi, "Come, how foolish he looks. What is he doing . . . ?" whispered one. "That's no way to dig . . ."

The other sneered, "He has no idea what he is doing . . . You can clearly tell . . . But that's how it is when people do things they do not understand."

Bambi suddenly stopped, threw up his head, listened closely, and peered through the bushes. There was something shimmering that caught his eye, a red spot through all the twigs, and above it he spied the unmistakable points of a crown. Bambi snorted. Whoever was roaming about there, Ronno or Karus or someone else—attack! Bambi dashed over. *"I'll show them that I am not afraid!"* he thought, suddenly as if he was in a stupor, *"I'll show them that I am the one they ought to be afraid of!"*

The bushes rustled with the swiftness of his attack, the branches cracked and broke. Bambi could now see his target was close by, but he was too hurried to recognize him as everything swam in front of his eyes. He thought of nothing else but, *"there, go get it!"* He lowered his crown, stormed forward, and braced his neck, ready for the shock of impact. Already he could sense the odor of his target, but he saw nothing more than the red wall of his flank. Then his target made a very slight movement and Bambi, hardly expecting or intuiting this move, rushed past him into the void. He almost fell over. He staggered, pulled himself together, and turned back to attack anew.

It was then that he recognized the Old One.

Bambi was so surprised that he stood there shocked. He was ashamed, too ashamed to just run away as he wanted to. He was too ashamed to stay, but he did not move.

"Well . . . ?" asked the Old One, quietly. His deep voice that was so calm and commanding always cut through Bambi's heart. He was silent.

The Old One repeated himself, "Well . . . ?"

"I thought . . ." stammered Bambi, ". . . I . . . thought . . . Ronno . . . or . . ." Again, he was silent and barely mustered the strength to look at him, which made him even more confused.

The Old One stood motionless and powerful. His head had turned white, and his dark, proud eyes shone deeply.

"Why not fight me . . . ?" asked the Old One.

Bambi looked at him and was filled with a strange fascination and a mysterious shudder ran through is body. He wanted to call out, *"For I love you!"* but instead he answered, "I don't know . . ."

The Old One looked at him. "I have not seen you for some time. You have grown large and strong."

Bambi said nothing. He trembled with joy.

The Old One continued to look him over. Then, surprisingly, he came close to Bambi, which frightened him.

"Behave yourself . . ." said the Old One.

He turned away, and in a moment had disappeared. Bambi stayed fixed to the spot for some time.

CHAPTER 13

It was summer and burning hot. A desire began to rise in Bambi once more; he had felt it before, but this time was much stronger than the last time. It boiled his blood and made him restless.

He wandered far.

One day, he met Faline quite unexpectedly. Quite unexpectedly, for his thoughts were very confused at the time, his senses so fogged by the restless longing that he did not notice Faline at first. Now she stood before him. Bambi looked at her speechlessly for a while, then said he spoke, suddenly, "Faline . . . how beautiful have you become . . ."

Faline responded, "Do you recognize me then?"

"How could I not recognize you?" said Bambi. "We grew up together!"

Faline sighed, "We have not seen each other for so long . . ." Then she added, ". . . Sometimes we grow apart and don't recognize others," but now her tone had become lighter, daintily teasing as when they were young.

"This path here," said Bambi after some time, "was where I walked with my mother as a child . . ."

"Yes, it leads to the meadow," she said.

"The meadow is where I first saw you," said Bambi, with a bit of joy in his voice. "Do you still remember that?"

"Yes," replied Faline, "Where you met Gobo and me." She sighed gently, "Poor Gobo."

Bambi repeated, "Poor Gobo."

They spoke of those days, asking each other every time, "Do you remember that?" It seemed that they still both remembered everything. That made them both glad.

"Out there on the meadow," recounted Bambi, "Was where we played tag . . . Do you remember that?"

"I think so, like this . . ." said Faline and darted off like a bolt of lightning. At first, Bambi just stood there, quite confused, and then ran after her. "Wait! Wait!" he called out happily.

"I won't wait," teased Faline, "I am in quite a rush!" She dashed in an arch farther into the bushes and grass. Finally, Bambi caught up to her and blocked her path, and then they stood there, calmly. They laughed and were happy.

Suddenly, Faline leapt into the air as if something had pricked her and she then ran off again. Bambi chased after her. Faline curved this way and that, turned around and managed to get away every time.

"Wait, stop!" panted Bambi. "Stop for a moment . . . I have to ask you something."

Faline stopped. "What do you have to ask me?" she asked curiously.

Bambi said nothing.

"Ah, if you just tricked me . . ." said Faline sassily and looked as if she would leave.

"No!" Bambi spoke quickly, "Just wait a moment . . . I want . . . I want to ask you . . . do you love me, Faline?"

She looked at him with more curiosity than before and a bit slyly, "I don't know."

"Oh come," pleaded Bambi, "You have to know! I know it, I can feel it clearly—that I love you. I love you madly, Faline. So, tell me if you love me too."

"I certainly think that I care about you," she answered.

"And will you stay with me?" Bambi pressed on.

"If you ask me too," said Faline joyfully.

"Yes, I am asking you, Faline! Dear, beautiful Faline," called Bambi out loud, "Can you hear me? I am asking you, pleading with my entire heart!"

"Well then yes, of course I will stay with you," Faline spoke softly—and she was gone.

Bambi whistled with joy as he ran after her. Faline ran in sweeping arches over the meadow, turned a corner, and disappeared in the thicket. But as Bambi rounded the corner to follow after her, a loud noise came from the bushes and out jumped Karus.

"Stop!" he called.

Bambi was confused. He was trying to find Faline and had no time for distractions. "Let me pass," he said hastily, "I have no time for you now!"

"Get out of here!" Karus growled at him. "Right now! Otherwise I will chase you until you run out of breath! I forbid you to follow Faline!"

Bambi remembered the previous summer when he had been chased away so often and so miserably. Now he was furious. He said nothing, but lowered his crown and threw himself at Karus.

The impact was powerful and Karus lay in the grass before he even realized what had happened. He stood back up quickly, but no sooner was he on his feet than a new blow struck him; he staggered.

"Bambi!" He tried to call out again, "Bam—" but a third blow slid off his shoulder blade and he could hardly breath from the pain.

Karus jumped aside to escape Bambi who again came raging at him. He suddenly felt strangely weak, yet at the same time he realized with horror that it was now death and life. Cold fear seized him. He turned to flee, and Bambi charged again in silence, close behind him. Then Karus realized that Bambi was out of his mind, angry and determined to kill him. This shocked him so. He stepped out of the way and used the last of his energy to break through the bushes, wanting and thinking of nothing more than mercy or safety.

Bambi paused, relaxed his stance, and stood there. Karus hardly noticed this in his fear and ran off through the bushes as best he could.

Bambi stayed there, standing still because he heard Faline's faint call. He strained his ears—there it was again, filled with fear and threat. He sped off.

As he arrived on the meadow, he saw Faline was fleeing into the thicket, followed by Ronno.

"Ronno!" called Bambi. He didn't know he had called.

Ronno, who could not run so fast as he still limped, stopped.

"Why look who it is," said he proudly, "the little Bambi! Do you want something?"

"I want," Bambi spoke calmly, but his voice was now different, with restrained power and controlled anger, "I want you to leave Faline in peace and for you to leave now."

"Nothing else?" taunted Ronno. "What a rude boy you have become . . . I never expected that."

"Ronno," said Bambi even quieter now, "I don't want to hurt you. For if you do not go now, right away, you will want to walk on your legs, but you won't be able to walk anymore . . ."

"Oh-oh!" called Ronno outraged. "Now this is how you speak with me? Because I limp? Well it is hardly noticeable anymore. Or do you think that even I am afraid of you, just because Karus was so pitifully afraid? I will give you some good advice . . ."

"No, Ronno," Bambi interrupted him, "I am the one that is giving you the advice. Leave now!" His voice shook. "You were always good to me, Ronno. I always thought you were very smart and I respected you, because you were older than I. Now I am saying this for the last time, leave now . . . I have no more patience . . . !"

"It's too bad," said Ronno scornfully, "that you don't have much patience. Oh, that is too bad for you, my young boy. But don't worry, I will be done with you quickly. You don't have to wait too long. Or did you forget how many times I have driven you off before?"

With these words, Bambi waited not a moment longer. He rushed at Ronno like mad and Ronno received him with a bowed head. They crashed. Ronno stood firmly, surprised that Bambi did not back off, but the sudden attack had also baffled him. He had not expected Bambi to attack him first. The pain from Bambi's giant strength jarred him, and he took a moment. He wanted to use a trick, as they stood face to face with their crowns interlocked. Suddenly, he gave in, backing away, so that Bambi would lose his balance and stumble forward.

But Bambi reared up on his back legs and threw himself with all his might upon Ronno, leaving Ronno no time to get a strong stance. There was a bright, crackling noise as a point on Ronno's crown splintered. Ronno thought his skull was shattered. Sparks flew in front of his eyes, and his ears rang. The next moment, a huge blow tore his shoulder. His breath stopped, he lay on the ground, and Bambi stood angrily over him.

"Let me go," groaned Ronno.

Bambi struck without looking. His eyes sparked. He seemed to not even think of sparing him.

"I beg you . . . please stop," said Ronno with desperation. "You know that I limp . . . I thought that it was all a joke . . . spare me . . . don't you know it was a joke . . . ?"

Bambi let him go without saying a word. With great effort, Ronno stood up. He was bleeding and swayed uneasily on his legs. He said nothing and retreated.

Bambi wanted to go into the thicket to look for Faline. Just then she came out. She had been standing on the edge of the forest and had seen everything. "What a fight," she said. She was serious and quietly added, "I love you."

And so, they wandered off together and lived happily.

CHAPTER 14

One day, they were on their way to seek out the clearing deep in the forest where Bambi had last met the Old One. Bambi told Faline enthusiastically all about him.

"Maybe we'll meet him again, I think about him so often."

"That would be nice," said Faline boldly, "I would really like to chat with him once." This was not the truth, however, for she was curious about the Old One, but also afraid of him.

Dawn was coming; the sky began to turn a light grey. The sun would rise soon.

They walked next to each other where the shrubs and boughs were spaced out and one could see all around. Not far from them, there was a noise. They stopped immediately and looked about. There a deer strode slowly and mightily through the bushes and into the clearing. The pale twilight only showed a large grey shadow.

Faline could not stifle her scream. Bambi kept calm. He was just as shocked, but he stopped his yell in his throat. The helpless sound Faline let out made him feel great sympathy and he wanted to comfort her.

"What is wrong, calm yourself!" he whispered with care, but his voice wavered. "What is it? He'll do us no harm!"

Faline bleated once more.

"Come, don't get so terribly worked up, my love," Bambi pleaded. "How silly to be afraid by this buck, for he is one of our kind."

But Faline wanted to hear nothing of it. She stood there frozen and stared at the buck who calmly walked on, and she frantically bleated and bleated.

"Calm down," begged Bambi, "What will he think of us?"

Faline could not be calmed. "He can think what he wants," she called and yelled again, "*Ah-oh! Ba-oh!* . . . such nonsense to be so large!"

She continued on, "*Ba-oh!*" and on again, "Leave me be . . . I can't help it! I must! *Ba-oh! Ba-oh! Ba-oh!*" she bleated.

The buck now stood in the clearing and searched in the grass for something to eat.

Something stirred in Bambi as he looked from Faline to the quiet buck. He had overcome his fear by calming Faline. Now he scolded himself for feeling some fear as he looked over at the deer. Each time, it was the same mix of agony, horror, excitement, and wonder and calm which he felt.

"What nonsense," he said with determination, "I am going to go over there and introduce myself."

"Don't do that!" yelped Faline. "Don't do that! *Ba-oh!* Something terrible will happen, *ba-oh!*"

"I will do it," insisted Bambi. The buck who stood there calmly eating, ignoring the whining Faline, was too much for him. He felt somewhat displeased and embarrassed. "I am going," he said. "Be quiet now! Nothing will happen, you'll see. Wait here."

He then left. But Faline did not wait. She couldn't stand to and she was too afraid. She turned and ran away yelling.

She thought it was the best—rather all she could do. As she got further and further away, she could still be heard, *"Ba-oh! Ba-oh!"*

Bambi would have happily followed, but that was not quite possible. He composed himself and stepped forwards. He saw the buck standing there in the opening through the branches, his head was bent down to the ground. Bambi felt his heart pounding as he stepped out.

Immediately, the buck lifted his head up high and looked over. He seemed to look straight ahead, as if distracted.

Bambi thought that was also quite arrogant of him, the way that the buck looked at him, the way he just stared off as if no one was standing there.

Bambi did not know what he should do. He had come out into the opening just to speak with the buck. *"Good morning,"* he would say. *"My name is Bambi . . . may I ask your name?"*

He thought it would be very easy and now it seemed very complicated. How should he begin? Bambi did not want to be rude, but that is what he was being if he would come out here and not say a thing. He also did not want to be too nosy, which he was being if he'd just approach him.

The buck stood there so majestically. Bambi was entranced and humiliated. In vain, he tried to push himself on, but again and again, he just repeated one thought in his mind, *"Why am I being so shy? I am just as grand he is . . . just as much as he is!"*

It did not help. Bambi stood there, shy, and he felt as if he wasn't so grand. Not at all. He felt miserable, and he needed all his strength to stay calm.

The buck looked at him and thought, *"He is fantastic . . . he is really quite majestic . . . so handsome . . . so graceful . . . so well-mannered . . . but I cannot stare at him so. That won't do. What if that embarrasses him?"*

So, he stared off beyond Bambi at nothing in particular.

"*This haughty look!*" thought Bambi. "*How unbearably proud he must be!*"

The buck thought, "*I would like so very much to speak with him . . . he seems so kind . . . how silly that we deer never speak with one another!*" And he looked off into the distance, as if deep in thought.

"*What, am I just air?*" thought Bambi, "*Oh, how we deer just pretend to be so alone in the world!*"

"*But what should I say to him . . . ?*" thought the buck, "*. . . I have never done this before . . . what if I say something stupid and he laughs at me . . . I imagine he is very smart.*"

Bambi tried to gather his courage and looked directly at the buck. "*How magnificent he is!*" he thought, confused.

"*Well maybe another time . . .*" thought the buck and walked away, unhappy, but glorious.

Bambi remained there, feeling bitter.

CHAPTER 15

The forest was so hot from the scorching sun. Since she had risen, she had drunk up all the clouds and now she was all alone in the vast blue sky which grew pale in the heat. Over the meadows and the treetops, the air trembled in glassy, transparent waves as it trembles over a flame. Not a single leaf moved, nor a blade of grass. The birds remained silent, hiding in the shade of the trees, and did not move. Every path and trail in the thicket was empty, for no animals were about. The forest lay motionless in the blinding light, paralyzed. The earth, the trees, the shrubs, and animals breathed in the heavy blaze of the heat. Bambi slept.

The whole night he had been happy with Faline; they had explored until the bright morning came and they had even forgotten to eat in their bliss. But then he had become so tired that he didn't even feel hungry. His eyes drooped shut. Wherever he found himself, he lay down in the middle of the bushes and fell asleep immediately. The bitter-sharp smell that the juniper gave off when inflamed by the sun, and the fine scent of the young garland flower near his head filled him as he slept and gave him new strength.

Suddenly, he awoke and was confused.

Wasn't that Faline calling?

Bambi looked around him. He could remember that Faline had stood close to him—by the hawthorn—and picked leaves as he slept. He thought she would stay there, but as he awoke he saw she was gone. She was probably bored of being alone and had called to him so that he would go and find her. As Bambi listened, he thought that he must have slept for some time, and wondered how often Faline must have called for him. He had no clue. His head was foggy from the veil of sleep.

There, he heard her call again. Bambi turned to the side where he had heard it come from. There it was again! And now he was overcome with joy. He felt refreshed, felt renewed and strong, and quite hungry.

The call rang out brightly once more, fine as quiet chirping, wistful and tender, "Come . . . Come . . ."

Yes, that was her voice! It was Faline! Bambi ran off quickly through the dry twigs of the bushes; as he broke through they rustled, and the hot, green leaves crackled.

Mid-jump, he noticed something off to the side and turned his head to look. There stood the Old One, standing on a path.

Love and admiration stirred within Bambi, but he wanted to pay the Old One no attention. He would surely see him again sometime. Now he had no time for distractions, even noble ones. Now he could only think of Faline.

He greeted him quickly and wanted to continue on.

"Where are you going?" asked the Old One, with a serious tone.

Bambi was a bit ashamed, searched for an excuse, but came up with nothing and answered honestly, "To her."

"Do not go," said the Old One.

For a moment he felt a flicker of anger, just for a moment. Not go to Faline? How could the Old One demand such a thing? Bambi thought, *I will just run away from him.*" He looked at the Old One quickly, but he stared with a stern gaze from his old eyes and Bambi could not move. He twitched impatiently but did not move from his spot.

"She is calling for me . . ." he tried to explain. He said it with a tone that made clear that he did not want to be held up.

"No," said the Old One. "She is not calling you."

A soft call echoed again, just like birds chirping, "Come!"

"There it was again!" called Bambi irritated. "Didn't you hear it?"

"I did," the Old One nodded.

"Well, then farewell . . ." spat Bambi quickly, but the Old One scolded him, "Stay here!"

"What do you want from me?" yelled Bambi, infuriated. "Let me go! I have no time for this. I am begging you . . . when Faline calls for me . . . you must understand . . ."

"I am telling you," the Old One spoke slowly. "It is not her."

Bambi was confused, "But . . . I know it is her voice . . ."

"Listen to me," continued the Old One calmly.

There, she called again.

The ground beneath Bambi burned. "No, I will come back later! I must go."

"No," said the Old One sadly. "If you go, you will not return. Never again."

They heard the call once more.

"I must . . . I must!" Bambi was about to go mad.

"Very well," agreed the Old One, "then we will go together."

"Fine, but hurry!" called Bambi and prepared to leap.

"No . . . slowly!" commanded the Old One with a voice that Bambi could not disobey. "You will follow behind me. Step for step . . ."

The Old One began to move forward and Bambi followed impatiently, sighing loudly.

"Listen," said the Old One, as he continued walking. "No matter how often it calls, do not leave my side. If it is Faline, we will find her soon enough. If it is not Faline . . . you must control yourself. Everything depends on whether or not you trust me."

Bambi could not object.

The Old One proceeded slowly and Bambi followed. Oh, how quietly the Old One could move through the forest! Not a single sound was made by his careful steps. No leaf nor twig dared make a sound. He moved through the thickest growths, the oldest branches. Bambi was astonished and amazed, in spite of his feverish impatience. He had never thought that it was possible to move so quietly.

Again, it called out—once, twice.

Now the Old One stopped, listened, and nodded.

Bambi stood next to him, though he longed to go to Faline.

The Old One stopped many times, even if there was no call, and lifted his head up high, listened, and then nodded. Bambi heard nothing. The Old One turned away from the calls and started to walk in a wide arch. This angered Bambi.

It called out again.

Finally, they got closer, closer, and then very close to where the calls came from.

The Old One whispered, "No matter what you see now . . . you must not move . . . do you understand? Pay attention to everything that I do, every move. Do just as I do . . . Be careful! And stay calm!"

A few steps later, suddenly there was a sharp smell in the air that Bambi knew all too well. He swallowed so much of it that he almost shrieked. He stopped in his tracks. His heart beat so hard, it felt like it rose up into his throat.

The Old One stood calmly next to him. His eyes however gave a clear command . . . There!

There it was . . . there *He* stood!

He stood very close to them, up against the trunk of an oak tree and covered with hazel bush, and called out quietly, "Come . . . Come . . ."

His back was visible, his face mostly hidden, only visible when he turned to the side.

Bambi was confused, he was so shocked that he only slowly came to understand that it was not Faline's voice he heard, but that *He* was whistling her call, "Come . . . Come . . ."

A sensation of terror ran through Bambi's limbs. The desire to run tugged at his heart.

"Be quiet!" whispered the Old One, hastily and sternly, as if he could stop Bambi's instincts with his words. Bambi tried with all his might to remain still and calm. The Old One looked at him, scornfully at first, but then with earnest and goodwill.

Bambi peered over where He stood and felt as if he could no longer endure this terrible presence.

As if the Old One had read his thoughts, he whispered, "Let's go . . ." and turned away.

They crept away cautiously, the Old One leading in a strange, zigzag path, the purpose of which Bambi did not understand. Still he followed in his slow steps with laboriously controlled impatience. Until now he had been driven by the desire to see Faline, but now it was the instinct to escape that coursed through his veins.

The Old One continued on slowly, stopped for a moment, listening intently, and then changed the direction of their zigzagging path, stopped again, and waited a moment before continuing on ever so slowly, so very slowly.

By now they must have been far away from the place they had seen Him.

"If He stays where He is, and I thank Him if He does, then it is now safe," spoke the Old one and immediately disappeared in a jumble of high dogwood bushes. As he slipped through, not a leaf moved, no twig snapped.

Bambi followed and tried to be as silent and artfully avoid making a sound, but alas he was not as graceful; the leaves rustled, the branches brushed against his sides, and dry twigs snapped with short, creaking crunches.

"Why, he saved my life," thought Bambi. "What can I say to him?"

But the Old One was nowhere to be found. Bambi stepped cautiously out from the bushes and found himself in a glowing field of goldenrod. He lifted his head and looked all around for a sign of the Old One. Not a single straw moved as far as he could see. He was alone.

He felt free and needed no longer suppress his urge to flee, but still he tore off instantly. The goldenrod made a swishing noise as he dashed in long bounds across the field. After searching everywhere for some time, he finally found Faline. He was out of breath and exhausted, but happy and deeply moved.

"I beg you, my love," he said, "I beg you . . . do not call out for me when we are separated . . . never call for me again . . . ! We shall search until we find each other . . . but I beg of you, do not call after me, for I cannot resist your call."

CHAPTER 16

A few days later, they wandered carefree amidst the oak trees that stood across the meadow. They wanted to cross over the meadow where the largest oak stood to return to their familiar path. Suddenly, the bushes ahead of them were brighter; they stopped and observed. Over by the oak tree moved something that was red.

"Who could that be . . . ?" whispered Bambi.

"Probably Ronno or Karus," said Faline.

Bambi doubted it. "They would not dare come close." Bambi looked even closer. "No," he said decidedly, "that is certainly not either of them . . . that is a stranger . . ."

Faline agreed, surprised and curious. "You're right, a stranger, I can tell too . . . how peculiar!"

They both watched.

"How strange he behaves!" called Faline.

"Dumb," said Bambi. "Really, quite dumb. He acts like a small child . . . he is not even being cautious!"

"Let's go over," suggested Faline. She was too curious.

"Fine," agreed Bambi, "we'll go . . . I have to get a closer look at him . . ."

They took a few steps forward, but Faline stopped short, "But . . . what if he wants to start a fight with you . . . ? He looks strong . . ."

"Bah!" Bambi held his head higher and made a disdainful face. "Look at his small crown of antlers . . . should I be afraid of that . . . ? He is round and fat . . . but strong? I don't believe so. Come on, now . . ."

They continued.

The stranger was too busy chewing grass blades to notice they were coming. He only first saw them once they were a ways out into the meadow. Immediately, he came bounding over to them. He jumped about in a joyous, playful way that seemed very childish. Bambi and Faline stood confused and let him approach them. Soon he stood a few steps away and then also stood still.

After a while he asked, "Don't you recognize me?"

Bambi had bent his head, ready for an attack. "Do you . . . know us?" he retorted.

The other cut him off. "Of course, Bambi!" he called, taunting and familiarly.

Bambi was startled to hear his name. Something in the sound of this voice tugged at memories in his heart, and in that moment Faline had already jumped towards the stranger.

"Gobo!" she called out and quickly fell silent. She stood there, breathless.

"Faline . . ." said Gobo quietly, "Faline . . . sister . . . you *do* recognize me . . ." He came over to her and kissed her on the cheek. Suddenly, tears ran down his cheeks.

Faline cried too and could not speak.

"Oh my . . . Gobo . . ." Bambi began, but his voice shuddered.

He was both touched and astounded beyond all measure. "My dear . . . Gobo . . . you survived . . . ?"

Gobo laughed. "As you see . . . yes, I survived . . . I think you can surely tell that."

"But . . . back then . . . in the snow?" Bambi asked, confused.

"Oh, back then?" Gobo shook himself. "Well, back then He saved me . . ."

"And where were you all that time . . . ?" asked Faline in complete confusion.

Gobo replied, "Well, with Him . . . the entire time I was with Him . . ."

He was silent; he looked at Faline and Bambi, enjoying their perplexed amazement. Then he added, "Yes indeed . . . all the things I have seen . . . more than all of you have here in your forest . . ." It sounded a bit boastful, but they did not notice that as they were still too dizzy from the big surprise.

"Oh, do tell us everything!" demanded Faline with great excitement.

"Well," Gobo was pleased, "I could tell you stories for days and days, and still have stories!"

Bambi urged him on, "Well then tell us!"

Gobo turned to Faline and became stern, "Is mother still alive?" he asked, timid and quiet.

"Yes!" answered Faline merrily. "She is alive . . . but I have not seen her in some time."

"I want to go to her!" said Gobo. "Will you come with me?"

Off they went together. They spoke not a word as they walked. Bambi and Faline could sense Gobo's impatient longing to see his mother, so they were both silent. Gobo walked hurriedly and was also silent. They left him in peace. Sometimes, when he blindly walked past a turn he should have taken, continuing straight, or if he suddenly changed directions, they would quietly direct him. "This way!" Bambi would whisper. Or Faline would say, "No . . . now this way . . ."

Sometimes they had to cross wide openings and Gobo never stopped for a moment, not even to check if the coast was clear. He did not pause at the edge of the thicket, and just walked out into the openness without caution or care. Bambi and Faline exchanged astonished glances each time he did so, but they said nothing and just followed Gobo with a bit more distance.

They had to walk for some time, this way and that. Suddenly, Gobo remembered the paths of his childhood once more. He was so moved, he didn't consider that Bambi and Faline had lead him this far. He looked around and called out, "Well what do you think, look how quickly I found the path!"

They said nothing, they just exchanged looks.

Soon after, they came to a small wooded opening. "Here!" called out Faline and slipped inside. Gobo followed her and stopped. It was the wooded den where both of them had been born, where they had lived as little children with their mother. Gobo and Faline looked closely into each other's eyes. They did not speak a word. Faline kissed his brother softly on the cheek. Then they hurried on.

They probably wandered about for another hour. The sun was getting brighter and lighter through the branches, the forest grew quieter and quieter. It was time to lie down and rest. But Gobo did not feel tired. He strode forward hastily, breathing with impatient excitement, and looking aimlessly around. He winced when a weasel scurried through the tufts of grass beneath him. He almost stepped on the pheasants, huddled close to the ground. But when they flew up in front of him with a rush of flapping wings, scolding loudly, he was startled. Bambi was concerned at how strange and blind Gobo wandered along.

Gobo stopped and turned to them. "Nowhere to be found!" he called out, confused.

Faline calmed him. "Soon," she said. "Soon, Gobo." She looked at him. He had that faint-hearted expression that she knew so well.

"Should we call after her?" she said, smiling. "Should we call again . . . like we did as children?"

Bambi continued on however. Just a few more steps. There he saw Aunt Ena. She had already found a spot to relax in the shadow of a hazel bush not far away.

"Finally!" he sighed. In that moment, Gobo and Faline arrived too. They all stood next to each other and looked over at Ena. She had lifted her head and looked over at them sleepily.

Gobo took a few timid steps forward and called quietly, "Mother!"

As if struck by lightning, she was up on her legs and stood strong. Gobo bounded over to her, "Mother . . ." he began again. He wanted to speak but could not make a sound.

His mother looked at him, deep into his eyes. His presence undid her. She began to shiver and shake in waves that ran over her shoulders and back.

She did not ask where he had been, she demanded no explanation or stories. She just slowly kissed him on his cheek, his forehead, and began to bathe him in kisses as she had done in the hour of his birth.

Bambi and Faline left.

CHAPTER 17

They stood together in the middle of the thicket in a small opening, and Gobo told them everything.

Even Friend Rabbit came to sit, his spoon-like ears raised up high as he listened intently, sometimes falling when he was overcome, only to be lifted up again.

Magpie perched on the lowest branches of the young beech tree and listened in amazement. Jay sat across from her in an ash tree, restlessly calling out from time to time. A few pheasants they knew well had come with their wives and children. They stretched their necks in wonder as they listened, recoiled occasionally, and turned their heads about, but stayed silent.

A squirrel had come by and was clearly quite anxious. He jumped down to the ground, then darted up this tree or that tree. Soon he leaned back against his beautiful, towering tail, exposing his white chest. Time after time, he wanted to interrupt Gobo, wanted to say something, but everyone shushed him.

Gobo told them all how he had lain helpless in the snow and waited for death.

"The dogs found me then," he said. "The dogs are terrible. They are the worst creatures in the entire world. Their throats are full of blood, their voices are full of anger and without mercy." He looked about the group and then continued on, ". . . Well . . . since then I have even played with them as if they were my own kind . . ." He was very proud of this. ". . . I don't need to be afraid of them, because we are friends. Still when they begin to get angry, something in my brain boils and my heart becomes rigid. They don't always mean to be so cruel—as I said, I am even their friend—but their voices have such a terrible violence in them." He fell silent.

"Go on!" urged Faline.

Gobo looked at her. "Well, back then, they would have ripped me to pieces . . . but then He came!"

Gobo paused. The others hardly breathed.

"Yes," said Gobo. "Then He came. He called his dogs off and they were immediately still. He called again, and they went to him and sat perfectly still before him. Then He came and picked me up. I yelled. He gently petted me. He held me tenderly against Him and did not hurt me. Then He carried me away . . ."

Faline interrupted him, "What is that, 'carried'?"

Gobo tried to explain it, simply and with importance.

"Quite simply," called Bambi, interrupting, "You see, Faline, like the squirrel does when he has a nut and wants to bring it with him . . ."

The squirrel could finally say something. ". . . A cousin of mine . . ." he began eagerly, but the others immediately scolded, "Quiet! Be quiet! Let Gobo keep telling his story!"

The squirrel had to be quiet. He was confused, and he pressed his front paws against his white chest, turned to Magpie, who sat next to him, and began to tell him, ". . . you see . . . a cousin of mine . . ."

But Magpie just turned her back.

Gobo told of wonders. "Outside it is cold and the storms howl. Inside with Him, it is windless and as warm as summer."

"Bah!" screeched Jay.

"It pours rain from the heavens and everything swims in water, but inside with Him there is not a drop and it is dry."

The pheasants cringed and turned their heads about.

"Outside, when the snows lay high, it was warm inside; sometimes it was quite hot, and He would give me hay to eat, chestnuts, potatoes, and beets . . . everything I could wish for . . ."

"Hay?!" Everyone called out at the same time, confused, in disbelief and shock.

"Fresh, sweet hay," Gobo repeated calmly, and looked around victoriously.

Squirrel snuck a few words in, "A cousin of mine . . ."

"Be quiet!" everyone called out.

Faline asked Gobo, "How did He have all these things, like hay in the winter?"

"He grows it," answered Gobo, "Whatever He needs, He grows. Whatever He wants, He has!"

Faline continued to ask, "But weren't you scared to be there with Him, Gobo?"

Gobo smiled proudly. "No, dear Faline. Not anymore. I knew that He did not want to hurt me. Why should I have been afraid? You all believe that He is evil. But He is not evil. If He loves someone, if you serve Him, He is good. Wonderfully good. No one in the world can be as good as Him . . ."

Suddenly, as Gobo spoke, the Old One silently appeared from within the bushes.

Gobo did not notice him and continued to tell his story. Everyone else had seen him though and held their breath in awe.

The Old One stood without moving and observed Gobo with a deep, stern gaze.

Gobo said, "Not just Him, but even His children loved me very much; also His wife and all the others. They would pet me, feed me, and play with me . . ." he stopped abruptly. He had seen the Old One.

A stillness fell over them.

Then the Old One asked in a calm, dignified voice, "What is that mark around your neck?"

Everyone looked at it and noticed for the first time that here was a dark line where his fur was pressed flat about his neck.

Gobo answered nervously, "That . . . ? That is from the band that I wore . . . it is His band . . . and . . . yes . . . and it is a great honor to wear His band . . . it is . . ." He became confused and stumbled on his words.

Everyone was silent. The Old One looked at Gobo for a long time with a piercing sadness.

"Unfortunate one," he said quietly, then turned and went away.

In the silent confusion that followed, the squirrel again began to chatter, "Well . . . a cousin of mine was also with Him . . . He had been captured and locked up . . . oh for a very long time, until one day, my cousin . . ."

But no one listened to the squirrel. The crowd broke up.

CHAPTER 18

One day, Marena appeared again.

Back when Gobo had disappeared, she was almost full grown, but she had been scarce since then. Almost no one had seen her, as she kept to herself, away from the others.

She was quite thin and looked very young. She was serious and quiet, but gentler than all the others. Now she had heard from the squirrel, from Jay and Magpie, the thrush and the pheasant, that Gobo had come home and had experienced wonderful things. She came to see him. Gobo's mother was very proud and happy about the visit. Gobo's mother had become very proud of her good fortune. She celebrated the fact that the whole forest spoke of her son, she often mentioned her fame, and demanded that everyone should acknowledge that her Gobo was the smartest, the most capable, and the best.

"What do you think, Marena?" she asked. "What do you think of Gobo?" She hardly waited for an answer and kept speaking. "Do you still remember how Ms. Nettla used to say that he wasn't worth much, for he would just shiver a little in the cold . . . do you remember that still . . . or how she had declared to me that he would not have much joy in his life?"

"Well, you certainly were quite worried about Gobo," answered Marena.

"Oh, but those days have passed!" his mother said and was somewhat surprised that someone could even think of such things. "Oh, I just think that it is too bad that the poor Ms. Nettla isn't alive to see him now, to see what became of my Gobo!"

"Yes, poor Ms. Nettla," said Marena quietly, "It is such a pity."

Gobo was happy to hear how his mother praised him. It pleased him. He would stand there, and the praises felt like warm sunshine.

His mother continued to tell Marena, "Even the Old Crown Prince came to see Gobo . . ." she recounted, her voice just a celebratory and secretive whisper. "He has never, ever appeared like that . . . but because of Gobo he came!"

"Why did he say 'unfortunate' to me?" Gobo said in a displeased voice. "I want to know what that is supposed to mean!"

"Let it go," his mother calmed him. "He is indeed strange and curious."

But Gobo kept on, "I've been going over it in my head all day. Unfortunate! I am not unfortunate! I am quite fortunate! I have seen more, experienced more than all others. I know more about the world and I know life better than anyone here in the forest! What do you think, Marena?"

"Yes," she said, "No one can deny that."

From that day on, Marena and Gobo always stayed together.

CHAPTER 19

Bambi searched for the Old One. He spent many nights roaming the woods without Faline until the hour when the sun would rise and even into the first hours of dawn.

Sometimes he would go to Faline; sometimes he was as happy to be with her as in times past and would enjoy listening to her or going to the meadow or the edge of the thicket for a meal, but it was not always enough for him.

In the past, his time spent with Faline had rarely been interrupted with thoughts of the Old One. Now he was in search of the Old One, felt an inexplicable urgency to find him, the need to see him, and only thought of Faline once in a while. She could always spend time with him, as often as she wanted. But he had little desire to spend time with the others, with Gobo, with Aunt Ena. He avoided them when he could.

The word the Old One had called Gobo rang in Bambi's mind. He was strangely bothered by it. From the first day that Gobo returned it had bothered him. Bambi did not know why, but the sight of Gobo tormented him. Bambi was ashamed for Gobo without knowing why, and he feared for him. But when they were together, with the innocent, self-confident, cheerful, and haughty Gobo, that one word would return to his mind. Unfortunate. It always came back to him.

One dark night, however, as Bambi was reassuring the Tawny Owl that he had indeed startled him, he thought to ask him a question, "Do you perchance know where the Old One could be right now?"

The Tawny Owl cooed to himself, he hadn't the foggiest idea. But Bambi realized that the owl was not being straight with him.

"No," he said, "I cannot believe that. You are so smart and know everything that goes on in the forest . . . You certainly know where the Old One is."

The Tawny Owl, who was all fluffed up, now lay his feathers tightly against his body. "Of course, I know," he cooed even more quietly, "but I cannot say . . . No, I truly cannot say . . ."

Bambi began to beg, "I will not tell on you . . . how could I, for I adore you so . . ."

The Tawny Owl fluffed up his feathers again, so he resembled a soft, grey-brown ball, and rolled his wise, big eyes a little, as he always did when he was in a mood, and asked, "Ah-ha, so you do adore me? Why is that?"

Bambi did not hesitate. "For you are so wise," he said he sincerely, "and also so funny and friendly. And because you are so good at startling others. How clever it is to startle others, so very clever. I wish I could do that, it would be such a talent to have."

The Tawny Owl had sunk his beak deep within his feathers and was happy.

"Well," he said, "I know that the Old One does very much like you . . ."

"Do you really think so?" interjected Bambi, his heart began to beat joyfully.

"Yes, I really think so," answered Tawny Owl, "He does like you, that is why I think I can tell you where he is . . ." He pulled his feathers in tight against his body again and was suddenly quite thin. "Do you know the deep ditch where the willows stand?"

"Yes," Bambi nodded.

"Do you know the oak forest that stands on the other side?"

"No," admitted Bambi, "I have never been over to that side."

"So, pay close attention," whispered Tawny Owl. "On the other side of there is an oak forest. You must go through it. Then there will be bushes, many bushes: hazel, silver poplar, hawthorn, and wild privet. In the middle of all the bushes there is a beech that was toppled by the wind. You must look for it. There below . . . the way you will see it, you can certainly not see it as easily as I can from the sky. There lives the Old One. Under the stump . . . but do not tell him I told you!"

"Under the stump?"

"Yes!" The Tawny Owl laughed. "Just there below it; in the ground is a hollow protected by the old stump. There you will find him."

"Thank you," said Bambi sincerely. "I don't know if I will find him, but I thank you!"

He was gone immediately.

The Tawny Owl followed him silently and then began to screech, *"Uwee Uwee!"*

Bambi startled.

"Did I startle you?" asked the Tawny Owl.

"Yes . . ." stammered Bambi, this time he spoke the truth.

Tawny Owl cooed and said, "I just wanted to remind you— do not tell on me!"

"Of course, not!" vowed Bambi and bound off. As he reached the ditch, suddenly the Old One appeared out of the gloomy darkness before him, so silently and so suddenly that Bambi again was startled.

"You will not find me where you are headed," said the Old One.

Bambi said nothing.

"What do you want from me?" asked the Old One.

"Nothing . . ." stuttered Bambi. "Oh . . . nothing . . . forgive me . . ."

The Old One finally spoke after some time, he spoke mildly. "This is not the first time you have searched for me."

He waited. Bambi said nothing. The Old One continued, "Yesterday you passed close by me twice and two more times this morning . . ."

"Why . . ." Bambi summoned his courage, "Why did you say that to Gobo . . . ?"

"Do you think I was wrong?"

"No," Bambi passionately answered, "No, I believe it is true!"

The Old One nodded so subtly and he looked at Bambi with a kindness he had never seen from him.

Bambi spoke, "But . . . why . . . ? I don't understand it!"

"It is enough that you feel it. You will understand it someday. Farewell."

CHAPTER 20

Everyone soon realized that Gobo had a strange and alarming habit. He slept at night when the others were awake and roaming about. During the day however, while the others searched for their hiding places to sleep, he was awake and wandered. He would walk out of a thicket without a moment's hesitation, when he wanted to, and stood calmly in the bright sunlight in the middle of the meadow.

Bambi could not stay silent any longer. "Don't you think about how dangerous it is?" he asked.

"No," answered Gobo simply, "There is no danger for me."

"You forget, my dear Bambi," Gobo's mother chimed in, "You forget that he is His friend. Gobo is allowed to do more than you or the rest of us." And she was quite proud. Bambi said nothing more. One day, Gobo commented to him, "You know, it seems strange to me that I can eat whenever I want and wherever I want here."

Bambi did not understand. "Why should that be strange? We all do that!"

"Yes . . . you all!" Gobo said, sounding superior, "But it is different for me. I am used to having my food brought to me, being called when it is ready."

Bambi looked at Gobo sympathetically, then looked at Aunt Ena, Faline, and Marena. But they all just smiled and marveled at Gobo.

"I believe," began Faline, "You will have a hard time getting used to the winter, Gobo. There won't be any hay or carrots or potatoes."

"That is true," pondered Gobo, "I had not thought of that. I can hardly imagine how it is. It must be terrible."

Bambi spoke calmly, "No, not terrible. It is just hard."

"Well," declared Gobo proudly, "if it is too hard for me, I will just go back to Him. Why should I go hungry? I really don't need to endure that."

Bambi turned without saying a word and walked away.

When Gobo was alone with Marena, he began to speak about Bambi. "He does not understand me," he said, "Our dear Bambi believes that I am still the dumb, little Gobo that I used to be. He cannot make peace with the fact that I am now something special. Danger! Why is he so concerned about danger? I am sure he only means well, but danger is something for him and his kind, not for me!"

Marena agreed with him. She loved him, and Gobo loved her, and they were very happy together.

"You see," he said to her, "no one understands me like you do. Well I shouldn't complain. I am generally respected and honored. But you understand me best. The others . . . even if I tell them now how good He is, they will listen to me—they certainly do not think that I am lying—but they still believe that He must be terrible! "

"I believe you," said Marena wistfully.

"So?" replied Gobo offhandedly.

"Do you remember," Marena said, "the day that you were laying in the snow? On that day I had said that He would come to us in the forest one day and play with us . . ."

"No," replied Gobo, "I don't remember that."

One morning, a few weeks later, Bambi and Faline, and Gobo and Marena sat together in their old familiar thicket of hazel bush. Bambi and Faline had just returned from roaming about when they passed the oak and were looking for a place to lay down when they saw Gobo and Marena. Gobo was just about to go out into the meadow.

"Oh, stay with us," said Bambi, "the sun will rise soon and then no one goes out into the meadow."

"Ridiculous," Gobo said mockingly, "If no one else will go . . . I will."

He took a step forward and Marena followed.

Bambi and Faline stopped. "Come!" said Bambi angrily to Faline. "Let him do as he wishes."

They wanted to go further. Something screeched on the other side of the meadow. A jay's warning.

Bambi immediately turned to run after Gobo. Just before the oak tree, he caught up to Gobo and Marena.

"Did you hear that?" he called he to Gobo.

"What?" asked Gobo, confused.

Jay called out his warning from the other side of the meadow once more.

"Did you hear that?" repeated Bambi.

"No," said Gobo calmly.

"It is dangerous!" Bambi spoke nervously.

Now a magpie piped up, followed by another, and then a third. In between, Jay continued shrieking, and from the sky above, a crow gave a call.

Even Faline began to beg him, "Do not go out there, Gobo! It is dangerous"

Even Marena begged, "Stay here! For me, my love, please stay here today . . . It is dangerous!"

Gobo stood there and laughed pompously. "Danger! Danger! What do I care?"

A thought came to Bambi in this moment of urgency, "Then let Marena go out first, so we know . . ."

He had not yet finished speaking and Marena had already slipped away.

All three stood and looked after her. Bambi and Faline were breathless. Gobo was obviously patient, as if he was tolerating the others' foolishness.

The watched Marena slowly enter the meadow, step by step, her head up high, legs slowly moving. She smelled and looked in every direction.

Suddenly, she turned in a flash, bounding back into the thicket with a powerful leap. "He . . . He is out there!" she whispered with a serious, choked voice. Her entire body quaked. "I . . . I . . . saw . . . Him . . . He . . . is there . . ." she stammered, "over there . . . by the alders . . ."

"Hurry!" called Bambi, "Run away, now!"

"Come!" pleaded Faline.

And Marena, who could hardly even whisper, said, "I beg you, Gobo, come now . . . please, I beg you . . ."

But Gobo stayed calm. "Run if you like, as far as you can." he said, "I won't stop you. If it is Him, I will go greet Him."

Gobo could not be stopped.

They all stayed, watched as he stepped out. They stayed, for his confidence compelled them to stay, and at the same time their tremendous fear for him had them frozen. They could not move.

Gobo stood out in the meadow and looked for the alders. He seemed to have found them and to have seen Him. There was a clap of thunder.

Gobo jumped at the bang, then suddenly turned and fled with hastened bounds back into the thicket.

They stood paralyzed by fear as he entered. They heard his wheezing breath, turned towards him, but he did not stop. Instead he ran past them in madness and they joined him in in fleeing.

But then Gobo collapsed.

Marena stopped immediately, standing right next to him. Bambi and Faline stood a bit further away, ready to flee.

Gobo lay there, his side torn open wide. He lifted his head in a dull movement.

"Marena . . ." he spoke with great effort, "Marena . . . He did not recognize me . . ." His voice cracked.

There was a reckless rustle in the bushes from the meadow.

Marena lowered her head to Gobo. "He is coming!" she whispered urgently. "Gobo . . . He is coming! Can't you stand up and come with me . . . ?"

Gobo again tried to move his neck but was too weak. He thrashed his legs and stayed there.

The bushes splintered, crackled, and rustled, and He entered.

Marena saw Him, so near. She darted off, disappeared behind a shrub, and rushed to Bambi and Faline.

She turned one more time and saw how He bent over the fallen Gobo and reached for him. Then she heard Gobo's pleading cry stop.

CHAPTER 21

Bambi was alone and walked to the water that flowed quietly between reeds.

He came here more often since he had started to keep to himself. There were few paths that led here, and he rarely saw his kind there. That was just how he wanted it. For now he had grown serious and his soul was heavy. He did not understand what was going on inside him, did not even think about it. He just brooded in confusion and it seemed to him that his whole life had become darker.

He spent many hours standing on the edge of the water. The gentle curves of the stream offered a nice view. The cool breath of the waves brought refreshingly crisp, strange odors that awoke carelessness and confidence within him. Bambi stood there and watched the ducks who floated by happily. They spoke incessantly—friendly, serious, and smart. There were a few mothers, and each had a flock of ducklings that were constantly and tirelessly learning. Sometimes there was a warning call from the mothers. Then the young ducks flew off in all directions; without hesitation, they separated in the sky, completely silent. Bambi saw for a moment how the little ones, unable to fly yet, drifted in the dense reeds cautiously, without touching a reed, so that they would not begin to wobble. Here and there he saw their small, dark bodies slowly disappearing in the rushes. Then he could not see them anymore. A quick call from the mother and in no time, they came back from all directions. They rushed in quickly and continued on as if nothing had happened. Each time it impressed Bambi as much as the first time. Such a feat!

Once, after a warning call, he asked one of the mothers, "What was the warning for? I was looking and saw no danger."

"There wasn't any," answered the duck.

Another time it was one of the ducklings who sounded the alarm and fast as lightning, they all went through the reeds and climbed up on the bank near to where Bambi stood.

Bambi asked the little duckling, "What happened? I didn't see anything."

"There was nothing," replied the young duckling. He shook off his feathers, carefully tucked his wings away, and went back into the water.

Bambi watched the ducks and realized that they were more attentive than he was, that they could hear and see better than he could. When he stood and watched, some of the tension in him disappeared.

He enjoyed speaking with the ducks. They didn't discuss the same things he had heard so often. They spoke of the open air, the wind, and distant fields where there were delicious treats.

Sometimes Bambi saw something small fly through the air near to the water; it looked like a fiery flash. "*Srrr-ih!*" a kingfisher called out quietly to himself as he snuck by. A small, buzzing dot, it glowed blue and green, flashed red and lit up, then disappeared. Bambi was amazed and wished he could get a closer look at it, and so he called after it.

"Don't even try," said a coot who was in the grass. "It won't answer you."

"Where are you?" asked Bambi as he looked about for the bird.

The coot laughed, he was somewhere far off from where Bambi looked. "Here I am! That grumpy one you were calling for . . . he won't answer you. It's pointless."

"He is so beautiful!" said Bambi.

"But so naughty!" retorted the coot, again from a different spot than before.

"Why do you say that?" inquired Bambi.

Again, the coot had moved elsewhere and answered, "He pays attention to no one and nothing. No matter what. He never says hello, or alerts anyone of danger. He has never spoken a word."

"The poor thing . . ." said Bambi.

The coot continued on in his merry voice, again from a different side of the stream, "He probably thinks that we are all jealous of his colors and does not want to be looked at closely."

"Well you won't show yourself either," said Bambi.

Suddenly, the coot stood before him. "There isn't much to see," he said simply. He was narrow, glistening from the water, and stood there in very plain black, with his graceful figure—restless, agile, cheerful. And whoosh, he was gone again.

"I don't understand how someone can stay in one place for so long," he called up from the water, again from somewhere else. Then he added, "It's boring and dangerous to stay in one place for so long." Again, from another place, he called brightly. "You have to move. If you want to live safely and find enough food, then you have to move!"

A quiet rustling in the grass startled Bambi. He looked about. There, on the bank, something shimmered red and disappeared in the reeds. At the same time a warm, sharp scent filled his nose. There was a fox sneaking about. Bambi wanted to shout and trample the ground to warn the animals, but suddenly there was a sound of crackling reeds, a splash in the water, and a duck screamed desperately. Bambi heard the flapping of her wings, saw her white body shimmering in the green growth, and saw wings whipping at the fox's cheeks. Then it became quiet.

Soon the fox came up onto the bank, holding a duck in his jaws. Her neck hung limp, her wings fluttered slightly, but the fox ignored it. He glared over at Bambi with mocking, cruel eyes and went off into the thicket.

Bambi stood still.

A few of the old ducks had taken off in stunned terror. The coot sounded its warning call in every direction. The titmice in the bushes twittered anxiously, and the young ducklings wobbled about in the reeds, crying in soft tones, abandoned.

The kingfisher crept along the bank.

"Please!" called the young ducklings, "Please, did you see our mother?"

"*Srrr-ih!*" called the kingfisher and snapped at them, "Leave me be!"

Bambi turned and left. He wandered through a thick wild field of goldenrod, amongst beech trees, crossed through old hazel bushes until he came to the edge of the large ditch. There he paced back and forth, hoping to meet the Old One. He had not seen him for a long time, since Gobo's demise. Then he saw him off in the distance and ran over to him.

They walked together in silence for some time. Then he asked Bambi, "Well . . . do the others still speak often of him?"

Bambi knew he spoke of Gobo and responded, "I don't

know . . . I spend most of my time alone now . . ." he paused, ". . . but . . . I think of him often."

"Is that so?" said the Old One, "Alone you say?"

"Yes," said Bambi expectantly, but the Old One was silent.

They continued on. Suddenly, the Old One stopped. "Do you hear something?"

Bambi listened. No, he heard nothing.

"Come!" called the Old One and hurried ahead. Bambi followed. Again, the Old One stopped. "Do you still not hear it?"

There, now Bambi could hear a strange sound that he did not recognize. It was like branches were being ripped off recklessly. Then something struck the ground, dull and irregular.

Bambi wanted to turn and run.

"Come!" called the Old One and ran in the direction of the noise. Bambi ran with him and dared ask, "Is it not dangerous there?"

"Yes!" answered the Old One darkly. "There is the worst danger!"

Soon they saw the branches that had been torn and shook, jerkily moving about. They walked over and noticed that there was a small path that went through the bush.

Friend Rabbit lay on the ground; he moved back and forth, wriggled, lay still again, wriggled, and with each movement, he was caught amongst strange twigs.

Bambi noticed something dark that was wrapped like a vine. It was twisted tightly, twisted about the twigs that were clenched around the rabbit, one above and one below his throat.

Friend Rabbit must have heard them coming. He tried to flee quickly, jumping up into the air, but fell, tried again to flee, tumbled down into the grass, and wriggled about.

"Stop moving!" commanded the Old One, and then with compassion and a soft voice that warmed Bambi's heart he spoke again. "Be calm, Friend Rabbit. It is I! Don't move now. Lie very still."

The rabbit lay motionless on the ground. His strangled breath rattled softly.

The Old One took the twig with the strange vine between his lips, pulled it off, stepped skillfully on it, held it firmly to the ground under his hard hooves, and then cracked it with a single blow of his crown.

Then he said to the rabbit, "Hold still, even if it hurts."

He tilted his head to one side, put a point of his crown close to the neck of the rabbit, pressed it firmly into his coat, behind his ears, poked and prodded. The rabbit began to squirm.

The Old One pulled back. "Be still!" he commanded. "This is a matter of life or death!" and he started over. The rabbit lay there, still and rattling. Bambi stood by, speechless.

Now, one point of the crown was pressed into the rabbit's fur beneath the trap. The Old One bent low, turned his head to push his crown in deeper and deeper into the trap until it finally loosed a bit, releasing slightly.

Air flooded into the rabbit's lungs, and with it his fear and pain came flowing in and out of him again. "Eeh . . . eeh . . . eeh!" he cried pitifully.

The Old One paused. "Be still," he spoke mildly. "Be still!" His mouth was close to the rabbit's shoulder, a point of his crown was between the rabbit's ears so that it appeared as if he had stabbed him.

"How can you be so foolish and cry now?" he murmured without severity. "Do you want to call the fox over to us? No? Well then, you must be quiet."

He continued to work slowly, carefully, to loosen the rest of the trap. Suddenly, it released fully. The rabbit slipped out and was free without realizing it. He took a step and then sat down, numb from the shock. Then he hopped off, slowly at first, shyly, and then gaining speed until he ran in wild jumps.

Bambi looked after him. "Not even a word of thanks!" he called, miffed.

"Oh, he is still in shock," said the Old One.

The trap lay there on the ground. Bambi kicked lightly at it. It rattled, and Bambi startled. This sound did not belong in the forest.

"From Him . . . ?" asked Bambi quietly. The Old One nodded.

They walked in close silence. "Beware," said the Old One, "if you go down a path, check the branches, check with your crown, here and there, up and down, and turn around if you hear that clinking sound again. When you have lost your crown, you must be even more careful. I haven't taken the paths for some time now."

Bambi sank into deep thought.

"He is not there . . ." he whispered, surprising himself.

The Old One answered, "No . . . He is not in the forest now."

"Still . . . Him!" Bambi shook his head.

The Old One continued on, his voice was bitter, "How did your Gobo explain it . . . ? Didn't he tell you all that He was all-powerful and gracious . . . ?"

Bambi whispered, "Is He not all-powerful?"

"As all-powerful as He is gracious," growled the Old One.

Bambi said with sadness, ". . . He was to Gobo . . . He had been gracious to him . . ."

The Old One stopped in his tracks. "Do you believe that, Bambi?" he asked sadly. For the first time he called Bambi by his name.

"I don't know!" called Bambi, tormented. "It makes no sense!"

The Old One said slowly, "One must learn to live . . . and be vigilant."

CHAPTER 22

A day came that caused Bambi great distress.

The first pale grey light of the dawn began to creep into the forest. There was a milky white fog over the meadow that slowly lifted, and the stillness lasted into the day.

The crows were not yet awake, nor the magpies or jays.

Bambi had seen Faline this morning. She was very sad and very shy.

"I am always alone," she said quietly.

"I, too, am also alone," replied Bambi hesitantly.

"Why don't you come to me anymore?" asked Faline shyly and it hurt him that his merry Faline had now become so stern and complacent.

"I must be alone," he said. No matter how hard he tried to say this gently, it sounded so harsh, even to him.

Faline looked at him and asked him so quietly, "Do you still love me?"

Bambi responded just as quietly, "I do not know."

Then she left him. There he now stood, alone underneath the great oak at the edge of the meadow, listening carefully, drinking in the morning wind, which was fresh; there were no dangerous smells, just the refreshing odor of wet earth, of dew and grass and damp wood. Bambi breathed in deeply. He suddenly felt very free, a sensation he had long forgotten. He excitedly entered the misty meadow.

There was a loud clap of thunder.

Bambi felt a horrific jolt, but it did not move him.

At breakneck speed, he bounded back into the thicket in fear and then ran further. He did not understand what happened; he could hardly form a thought, he just ran and ran. The shock had gripped his heart, his breath vanished as he rushed blindly onward. But suddenly he was struck by a stinging pain that he could not stand. He felt it running, hot, down his left leg. A thin burning thread that came from where the pain had first begun to stab. Bambi had to stop running. It forced him to slow until he felt as if he could no longer move his legs and he fell down.

How refreshing it was to lay there and relax.

"Get up! Bambi! Get up!" The Old One had appeared next to him and nudged his shoulder gently.

Bambi wanted to reply, "*I can't*," but the Old One said, "Get up! Get up!" with such urgency and tenderness in his voice that it calmed Bambi. The pain was silent for a moment.

Now the Old One spoke with hatred and anger, "Get up! You must get up now, my child!" *My child* . . . It was as if this had slipped from his lips, but Bambi stood up in no time.

"Good!" the Old One, exhaled deeply and then spoke urgently, "Come with me . . . do not stop . . . !"

He walked hastily. Bambi followed him, but he wanted so badly to fall to the ground, to lay and rest. The Old One seemed to know this and spoke to him without stopping. "Now, you must bear the pain . . . you cannot lay down, don't even think of it . . . not even for a moment, for even that will make you tired! Now you must save yourself . . . do you understand, Bambi? . . . Save yourself . . . or else you will be gone . . . Only think of going onward . . . that He is behind you . . . Do you understand, Bambi? . . . He will kill you without mercy . . . come along . . . just like that . . . always after me . . . it will work . . . it must work . . ." Bambi had no strength, not even to think. The pain wrestled within him with every step—stole his air and senses—and the burning strip that glowed hot down his leg caused him to feel euphoric.

The Old One made a large sweeping circle. It took some time. Bambi hardly noticed that they passed the great oak once more, for the pain was like a veil before his eyes, he was so weak.

The Old One stopped here and there to sniff the earth. "Here!" he whispered, "He . . . is here . . . and . . . there is a dog . . . come now . . . faster!"

They ran. But the Old One stopped again.

"See here . . . !" he called. "This is where you laid on the ground."

Bambi saw the impression of his body in the grass and a bright pool of his own blood.

The Old One smelled that spot in the grass with great care. "They have already been here . . . He and the dog . . ." he said. "Now, come on!" He walked slowly, always smelling the way.

Bambi saw the red drops on the leaves of the branches and glistening on the grass. "*We already came along this way,*" he thought, but he could not speak.

"Here!" said the Old One and was almost joyous, "now we are behind them . . ."

They followed the same trail for some time. Then they turned suddenly and began a new circle. Bambi followed in despair.

They came across the oak a second time, but from the other direction now. Then they passed the place where Bambi had fallen; this time the Old One took a new path.

"Here, eat this!" he commanded and stopped, brushing aside some grass to expose a few small leaves that were dark green, fat, and grew fresh out of the ground.

Bambi obeyed. It tasted so terribly bitter and smelled disgusting.

A few moments later, the Old One asked, "How are you?"

"Better," said Bambi quickly. He could speak now; his voice was clear, and his drowsiness subsided.

The Old One commanded him after a few more moments, "We must go on," and he walked behind Bambi for some time before saying, "Finally!" They stopped together. "Your blood has dried," the Old One spoke. "Your wound is not dripping, so you won't give us away anymore . . . He and His dog will not find you now."

The Old One looked very tired and exhausted, but in his voice was a brightness. "Come now," he continued, "You need to rest."

They made it to the wide ditch that Bambi had never crossed. The Old One walked into it, Bambi tried to follow him, but it took too much effort to climb up the other side. The pain began to grow again, and he stumbled, tried again, stumbled once more, and breathed heavily.

"I cannot help you," said the Old One, "you must come up here!" and with that Bambi managed to climb out of the ditch. He felt hot strips on his leg once more, he felt his energy slipping away for the second time.

"You are bleeding again," said the Old One, "I expected that. But it is just a little . . . and . . ." he lowered his voice, "it will not put us in danger anymore."

Slowly they walked through a hall of tall beech trees with

arched branches. The ground was soft and flat. It was easy to walk on and Bambi longed to lay down here, to stretch out and not move a limb. He could not continue any further. His head hurt, his ears rang, his nerves quaked, and he began to shake with fever. He began to feel lightheaded. He only felt the desire for calm and he was confused that his life had suddenly been interrupted and changed like this. That he had ever been healthy and walked through the forest unharmed . . . just this morning . . . not an hour ago . . . that now seemed like the happiness of a distant, far-off time.

They arrived at a thicket of low oaks and dogwood. There was a mighty, cracked oak stump that lay deep in in the bushes and blocked the path.

"Here we are . . ." Bambi heard the Old One say. He circled along the stump and Bambi followed him, almost falling into a ditch that was just alongside it.

"There!" said the Old One, "you can lay there."

Bambi sunk to the ground and moved not a bit.

It was like the small den; the ditch was quite deep and protected by the oak stump. The bushes around the edge of the ditch seemed to fold over the top and guard the area. He felt as if he had disappeared.

"You are safe here," said the Old One. "Stay here now."

Days passed.

Bambi lay in the warm earth with the edge of the fallen tree above him; he could hear the pain as it left his body—as it grew, and then became less again, becoming quieter and quieter. Sometimes he managed to crawl out, standing weakly and swaying on his unstable legs, taking a few stiff steps to look for food. He now ate herbs that he had always ignored or never even seen. Now, however, they seemed to call after him with their scent and strange, inciting sharpness. What he had turned his nose up at, what he had thrown away, now seemed delicious and tasty. Some small leaves, some short stalks were even now not appetizing, but he still ate them for that was all he found, and it healed his wounds faster. He could feel his energy coming back.

He was healed. He did not leave the ditch yet; he would barely move at night and during the day he stayed in his bed. At first, since his body felt no more pain, Bambi relived everything that happened once more in his thoughts and it startled him. A deep shock would wake him. He could not get away from it. He could not get up and walk around as usual. He lay there and was mad—he was alternately shocked, ashamed, astonished, touched, and full of sadness and then soon again of happiness.

The Old One always stayed with him. At the beginning, he was there day and night, always at Bambi's side. Now he let him be alone sometimes, especially when he noticed that Bambi had fallen into brooding. But he always came back.

One evening, after thunder and lightning and a storm, came a blue sky that was then lit up by the setting sun. All about the treetops sang the blackbirds and the finches; titmice whispered from the bushes and the crows called from the high grasses; the pheasants sounded their short calls from under branches in their metallic, bursting voices; the woodpecker laughed cheerily; and the pigeons cooed their heartfelt love.

Bambi came out of his ditch. Life was beautiful. The Old One stood there, as if he had been waiting.

They walked slowly with one another. They walked through other ditches, but Bambi never went back to his.

CHAPTER 23

One night, when the leaves began to whisper that autumn was coming, Tawny Owl yelled through the treetops. Then he waited. Bambi had spied him through the thinning foliage and stayed very still. Tawny Owl flew closer and called out louder. He waited. Bambi said nothing.

Tawny Owl could resist no longer.

"Aren't you startled?" asked he, displeased.

"Yes," replied Bambi gently. "A bit."

"So, so," cooed Tawny Owl, insulted, "Just a bit? I used to startle you so terribly. It was a real pleasure how shocked you were. Why aren't you shocked now . . ."

He was frustrated and repeated himself, "Just a bit . . ."

The Tawny Owl was old now, and so he was more vain and sensitive than ever.

Bambi wanted to reply, "*I wasn't shocked in the past, never, I just said it to make you happy.*" But he kept this to himself. He felt sorry for the good, old Tawny Owl, the way he sat there and got worked up. He tried to calm him down. "Maybe it's because I was just thinking of you," he said to Tawny Owl.

"What?" Tawny Owl cheered up at this. "What? You were thinking of me?"

"Yes," answered Bambi hesitantly. "Just now, as you began to screech. Otherwise I certainly would have been as frightened as I usually am."

"Really?" cooed Tawny Owl.

Bambi could not resist. What harm would it do? It really would please the little, old fellow.

"Really," he insisted, ". . . and am I glad . . . for when I suddenly hear you, a shock runs through me."

Tawny Owl ruffled up his feathers, turning into a soft, brown, and light grey, cloudy ball, and was very pleased. "That was very kind of you to think of me . . . very kind . . ." he delicately cooed. "We have not seen each other in some time."

"A very long time," said Bambi.

"I don't see you here on your old paths as much anymore," said Tawny Owl.

"No . . ." Bambi spoke slowly, "I don't take those paths much anymore."

"I, too have seen more of this big world lately," commented Tawny Owl with pride. He did not mention that his old stomping grounds were now taken over by rude, young creatures that had driven him out. "One cannot always stay in the same place," he added and waited for a response.

But Bambi had gone, he had now become just as good as the Old One at silently disappearing.

The Tawny Owl was indignant. "How rude . . ." he cooed to himself, rustled his feathers, dug his beak into his chest, and mused to himself, "It seems that a friendship with a noble gentleman is not a true friendship. Even if they are quite gracious . . . there comes a day when they will be rude . . . and then you sit there, dumb as I feel now . . ."

Suddenly, he dropped like a stone, straight to the ground.

He had spied a mouse, which now made one screech in Tawny Owl's beak before he tore the mouse to pieces, for he was filled with anger. Faster than usual, he ate the mouse up. Then he flew away. *"What is it about this Bambi that bothers me so?"* he thought. *"Why does this whole noble bunch bother me? Nothing at all matters to me!"* He started screaming; so piercing, so persistent, that a few wood pigeons, which he passed, awoke and had loud, wing-flapping fits on their roosts.

For many days, a storm swept through the forest and ripped the last leaves from the branches. Now the trees were very bare. Bambi walked back towards his ditch that he shared with the Old One in the soft, grey light before dawn to sleep.

A thin voice called after him quickly, two, then three times. He stood still. Squirrel bolted down from the branches and sat before him on the ground.

"It is really you!" he wheezed and staring at him with adoring wonderment. "I recognized you right away, just now when you walked past me, but I could hardly believe it . . ."

"What are you doing over here . . . ?" asked Bambi.

The joyful, little face in front of him suddenly turned worried. "The oak has fallen . . ." he began to complain, "my beautiful, old oak . . . Do you remember it? It was so terrible . . . He knocked it down."

Bambi's head fell with sadness. He mourned the beautiful, old tree.

"It happened so fast," Squirrel said. "All of us that lived on the tree had to flee and we stood there and watched as He bit through the tree with a huge, flashing tooth. The tree yelled out of the huge wound. He kept yelling, constantly . . . it was terrible to listen to. Then the poor, beautiful tree fell. Fell out into the meadow and we all cried."

Bambi was silent.

"Yes . . ." sighed Squirrel, "He can do anything . . . He is all-powerful . . ." He looked at Bambi with wide eyes and pricked up his ears, but Bambi was silent.

"Now we are all homeless . . ." Squirrel continued on. "I don't know where the others have gone . . . I came here, but I will never find a tree like that one again."

"The old oak . . ." said Bambi to himself. "I have known it since the days of my youth."

"But . . . it is really you!" Squirrel was again cheerful. "Everyone thought that you must be dead. Of course, some believe that you still live . . . sometimes there are stories that someone has seen you . . . but no one was ever quite certain, so we all thought they were just rumors . . ." Squirrel examined him carefully. "Well, of course . . . since you never came back again."

He sat there curiously, waiting for an answer.

Bambi was silent. But a silent, fearful curiosity stirred within him. He wanted to ask about Faline and Aunt Ena, Ronno and Karus, after all of the companions of his youth. But he was silent.

Squirrel still sat in in front of him and studied him. "Your crown!" he said full of admiration. "Such a crown! No one in the entire forest except for the great Old Crown Prince has such a magnificent crown!"

Not very long ago, Bambi would have been charmed and flattered by such a comment. Now he just stated, "Ah-ha . . . could be . . ."

Squirrel nodded vehemently. "Truly!" he said, "truly, you are even beginning to turn grey"

Bambi continued on.

Squirrel realized that the conversation was over, and swung through the twigs, "Good day," he called down, "And farewell! It was a pleasure. Should I see your old friends, I will tell them that you are alive . . . they will be glad to hear it."

Bambi heard this, felt a stirring in his heart. He said nothing. He had learned from the Old One when he was just a child. The Old One had taught him many things, many secrets throughout his life. And of all his teachings, the most important had been one must stay alone to survive, and if you understand the ways of life, if you want to learn great wisdom in life, you must stay alone!

"But," Bambi had once asked the Old One, "but we, we will always be together now, right . . . ?"

"Not for much longer," the Old One had replied.

That was just a few weeks ago.

Now he recalled this, and suddenly he remembered something else, the first words the Old One had spoken to him about being alone. Back when Bambi was just a small child and had called out for his mother, the Old One had come to him and asked, *"Can't you be alone?"*

CHAPTER 24

Once again, the forest floor was covered with snow and all the sounds of the forest were muted by its thick, white cover. Only the calls of the crows were audible, or now and then a worried magpie or shy titmouse would chatter. In time it grew even colder and then everything was silent. Then the air began to ring with the cold.

One morning the bark of a dog shattered the silence. It was a pesky, rushed barking that sounded throughout the forest, an overlapping clamor of sounds and echoing tones.

Bambi lifted his head and looked at the Old One who lay next to him in the ditch under the stump of the fallen beech tree.

"It does not concern us," the Old One responded to Bambi's expression.

Nevertheless, they both listened closely.

Where they lay in their pit, they were protected by the stump of the beech tree which was like a roof above them, the high snow kept the icy drafts of cold air away, and the tangled bushes hid them from any spying eyes.

The barking came closer, angry, panting, and heated. It must have been a small dog. It got closer and closer. Now they heard breathing from two animals, they heard a low, painful growl among the nasty growls. Bambi grew restless, but the Old One said again, "It does not concern us."

They stayed in their warm den and looked out at the surrounding world.

A crackling sound came closer and closer in the bushes; snow suddenly was knocked down from branches and a powdery dusting of snow floated in the air where it had fallen.

Now they could sense who was coming.

Through the snow and twigs and roots sprang, slipped, and crawled the old fox.

Just behind him, the dog broke through the woods. It was a small dog with short legs. Fox's front leg was shattered and above that his coat was torn open. He held the shattered leg up to look at it, the blood spurted from the wound; his breath whistled, and he stared, wide-eyed with fear and anger. He was desperate and exhausted.

He took a few steps, then turned back and went another direction, trying to confuse the dog.

But it found him still. The fox stood up on his hind legs. He could hardly move much more. He raised his injured front paw pitifully, with his jaws opened and his lip twitching, he hissed and snarled at the dog.

Immediately the dog replied, but his high-pitched, grating voice turned fuller and deeper.

"There!" he yelled. "There he is! There! There! There!" He was not scolding the fox, but clearly speaking to someone else who was far away.

Bambi knew, just as the Old One always had, that it was Him and that He had His hand with Him.

And the fox knew it too. His blood was streaming down

him now, pulsing from his chest on to the snow and forming a burnt red patch on the white icy blanket, which steamed softly.

A weakness had overcome the fox. His shattered paw sank powerlessly to the ground but was stung by a fiery pain at the touch of the cold snow. With difficulty, the fox picked it up again and held it trembling in front of his body

"Leave me be . . ." the fox started to speak. "Leave me . . ." he spoke quietly, pleading. He was pleading quietly, very weak and very humiliated.

"No! No! No!" the dog continued in his terrible howling.

"I beg of you . . ." said the fox, "I cannot walk . . . I am done for . . . Let me go . . . Leave me be . . . Let me return home and die in peace . . ."

"No! No! No!" howled the dog.

The fox became more insistent in his pleading. "But we are family . . ." he said, "practically brothers, we are . . . leave me to return home . . . please, let me die with my own kind . . . we . . . we are practically brothers . . . you and I . . ."

"No! No! No!" the dog terrorized him.

The fox now stood as high as he could. He could not hold his pointy snout up right and it dipped into his bloodied chest, though his eyes were still fixed on the dog. With an accusing voice, still bitter and sad, he asked, "Are you not ashamed of yourself . . . ? You traitor!"

"No! No! No!" yelled the dog still.

The fox, however, continued on, "You traitor . . . you renegade!" His torn body tensed up in hatred and contempt. "You are evil!" he hissed. "You miserable . . . you track us where He would never find us . . . You haunt us, where He cannot catch us . . . You deliver us . . . us, we are all your relatives . . . me, who is practically your brother . . . and you stand there and are not ashamed?

All at once, many voices called out from above them.

"Traitor!" called the magpies from the trees.

"Traitor!" squawked the jay.

"Hypocrite!" whistled the weasel.

"Betrayer!" hissed the polecat.

From all of the trees and bushes around them came hissing, shrieking, and scolding calls; the crows flying above began to screech, "Traitor!" They had hurried from their safe distance in the trees to hiding places on the ground. The indignant anger that had risen in the fox spread to them all, and the old, fierce anger in all of them—seeing his blood that pulsed down onto the snow and turn to steam before their eyes—made them furious and forget all fear.

The dog looked around and saw he was surrounded. "All of you!" he called. "What do you want? What do you know of anything? What are you even talking about? You all belong to Him just as I belong to Him. But I . . . I love Him, I worship Him! I serve Him! You all want to stand up to Him? You miserable ones, against Him? He is all-powerful! He is stronger than us! Everything that you have is from Him! Everything that grows here and lives here is from Him!" The dog shook from the frenzied energy.

"Traitor!" squealed the Squirrel.

"Yes!" hissed the Fox. "Traitor! No one other than you . . . You alone . . . !"

The dog danced about in crazed excitement. "I alone . . . ? You liar! Are there not many, many more with Him . . . ? The horse . . . the cow . . . the lamb . . . the chickens . . . from all of your families, there are some that are with Him and worship Him . . . and serve Him!"

"Rubbish!" snarled Fox with total disregard.

The dog could resist no longer and went for Fox's throat. Snarling, spitting, panting, they rolled in the snow, in a struggling, wildly snapping ball. Hair flew, the snow was kicked up, blood sprayed in fine drops. Fox could not fight long. He lasted just a few seconds, and he lay on his back, showing his light belly, twitching, stretching, and dying.

The dog shook him a few more times, then dropped him into the trampled snow, stood ready to attack again and called in a deep, deep voice, "There! There! There he is!"

Everyone had flown off in horror.

"Dreadful . . ." said Bambi quietly, back in his ditch to the Old One.

"Most horrific," replied the Old One. "They believe what the dog said, they believe they will spend their lives in fear; they hate Him and themselves . . . and they will die because of Him."

CHAPTER 25

The cold broke and in the middle of the winter was a pause. The earth drank up vast amounts of the melting snow and large areas of the dirt below began to show. The blackbirds had not yet begun to sing, but when they would fly down to the ground to search for worms, or when they would flutter from tree to tree, they would let out a long, happy call that was almost like a song. The woodpeckers began to chatter, the magpies and crows grew talkative, the titmice chirped happily with one another, and the pheasants had begun to flutter down from where they had slept to relax in a lovely spot of the morning sun, letting out their metallic call in chorus.

On such a morning, Bambi wandered farther than normal. In the first morning light, he reached the edge of the ditch. There on the other side, where he had once lived, he saw something stirring. Bambi stayed hidden in the bushes and spied from there. There was indeed someone, one of his kind that wandered slowly back and forth, searching amongst the spots of still frozen snow, looking for shoots of grass that were reaching up to the sky.

Just as Bambi wanted to turn about and leave, he realized it was Faline. His first instinct was bound over in her direction and to call after her, but he stayed put. He had not seen her for such a long time. His heart began to pound. Faline walked slowly, as if she was tired or sad. She now looked quite similar to her mother; *"a bit like Aunt Ena,"* Bambi thought to himself with a terrific, tormenting longing.

Faline lifted her head and sniffed about, as if she had sensed his presence. Again, Bambi wanted to move, to go to her, but he stayed where he was, swooning and motionless.

He saw that Faline had turned quite grey and was old. *"The cheerful and cheeky little Faline,"* he thought to himself, *"how beautiful she was and how agile she had been."* His youth flashed before his eyes. The meadow, the paths his mother had led him along, the joyous times spent playing with Gobo and Faline, the little grasshopper and butterfly, his fight with Karus and Ronno which had won him Faline's attention. He suddenly felt happy and was nevertheless shocked.

Across the way, Faline continued on with her head down to the ground, slow and sad. In this moment Bambi loved her with a rush of gentle melancholy and wanted to cross over the ditch that had separated them for so long and catch up to her. To speak to her and reminisce about the old times of their childhood.

He watched her all this time as she walked through the shrubs and eventually disappeared.

He stood there for some time and looked over where she had been.

A loud clap of thunder rang out. It startled Bambi.

It was here, on this side of the ditch.

The thunder sounded again and then again.

Bambi took a few cautious steps back into the thicket,

stopped there and sniffed the air. All seemed normal now. He slowly crept back home.

The Old One was already there but had not yet laid down. Instead, he stood next to the fallen beech stump, as if he had been waiting for Bambi.

"Where were you so long?" he asked so seriously that Bambi was silent.

"Did you hear that just now?" the Old One asked.

"Yes," answered Bambi, "Three times . . . He is in the forest."

"True . . ." the Old One nodded and repeated it with a special emphasis. "He is in the forest . . . we must go there . . ."

"Where?" said Bambi, confused.

"There," said the Old One and his voice was heavy. "There where He now is."

This startled Bambi.

"Do not startle so," the Old One continued, "Come now and without fear. I am happy that I can bring you there and show you this . . ." he paused, and then said quietly, ". . . before I depart."

Bambi looked sorrowfully at the Old One and saw how his health had declined. His head was now completely white, his face was thin, and the deep brilliance of his beautiful eyes was gone, in its place was now a weary, green shimmer, as if they were broken.

Bambi and the Old One did not go far before the first trace of that familiar, sharp scent that caused such rage and horror to well up in their hearts, wafted towards them. Bambi stopped. But the Old One continued on, straight towards the scent. Hesitantly, Bambi followed. The provocative smell came in ever-stronger waves. But the Old One continued on, undeterred. The thought of fleeing had again risen in Bambi, sprung into his throat, swelled in his chest, boiled in his head and limbs, trying to carry him away. He restrained himself and stayed behind the Old One

Now the scent was so powerful that there was nothing else he could sense, and it was almost impossible to breath.

"Over there!" said the Old One and turned off to the side.

Amidst broken twigs and churned up snow, there He lay on the ground, just two steps in front of them. A shriek escaped Bambi's lips and he jumped suddenly as if he would flee. He had never been so shocked in his life.

"Stop," he heard the Old One call, looked around him and saw the Old One stood, calmly, right next to Him.

In total amazement and compelled by his obedience, by boundless curiosity and quivering expectation, Bambi approached.

"Come closer . . . Have no fear," said the Old One. There He lay, His pale and naked face turned upwards, His hat further off in the snow, and Bambi, who knew nothing about hats, thought that His dreadful head had been broken two pieces.

His exposed throat was pierced by a wound that hung open like a small, red mouth. Blood still seeped out softly, blood in His hair, under His nose, lying in a pool in the snow that melted away from His warmth.

"Here we are," began the Old One softly. "We are standing right by His side . . . and where is the danger?"

Bambi lowered himself towards the body in the snow, the shape of which was mysterious and terrific. He looked into its broken eyes, which stared up towards him without looking at him and he was confused.

"Bambi," the Old One continued, "Do you remember what Gobo said, what the dog said, what everyone in the forest believed . . . do you remember?"

Bambi could not answer.

"Do you see, Bambi," he continued to speak. "Do you that He is laying there, just like one of us? Listen Bambi, He is not all-powerful, as they say. He is not the one who gives us everything that grows and lives here. He is not above us. He lays there next to us and just like us. He knows fear, the red, and pain, just as we do. He can be overpowered, just as we can. He now lays there, helpless, just like us, as you see here now. "

It was silent.

"Do you understand me, Bambi?" asked the Old One.

Bambi responded in a whisper, "I believe so . . ."

The Old One raised his voice, "Then speak!"

Bambi was moved and spoke with a trembling, but strong voice, "There is another one who is above us all . . . above all of us and above Him."

"Good, now I can go," said the Old One.

He turned to go and the two wandered together for some time.

In front of a high oak tree, the Old One stopped, "You cannot follow me now, Bambi," he began with a calm voice, "My time is up. Now I must look for a place for the last hour . . ."

Bambi wanted to speak.

"No," the Old One cut him off. "No . . . In this hour that I now must face, we are all alone. Farewell, my son . . . I loved you very much."

CHAPTER 26

A summer day dawned with a gentle glow; there was no wind, no cool mist. It seemed the sun had come up in a haste today, faster than normal. It quickly rose and brought its blinding flames, like an enormous fire.

The dew on the meadow and the bushes evaporated in no time and the earth became very dry, the dirt crumbled. It was quiet earlier than normal in the forest. Just the woodpecker could be heard, now and again, the occasional, tender coo of a pigeon.

Bambi stood in a small clearing, a rare open space in the deep thicket.

About his head, there buzzed a swarm of mosquitoes in the sun, singing and dancing.

There was a buzzing in the hazel bushes near Bambi. The buzzing came closer and then a may bug flew slowly past him, flew right through the swarm of mosquitoes, higher and higher, up to the tree tops where he would sleep until the evening. His wing case was opened and pointed out daintily, his wings hummed with great power. The swarm of mosquitoes parted to let him pass. His dark, brown body, wrapped in shivering glass-like wings, caught the sun as he disappeared.

"Did you see him . . . ?" the mosquitoes chattered to one another.

"That is the Old One," said someone.

And the others all sang, "All of his kind have died. But he still lives. He is alone."

A few very small mosquitoes asked, "How long will he live?"

The others answered in song, "We don't know. His kind lives very long. Almost for eternity, they live. Almost forever . . . They see the sun thirty, maybe forty times. We do not know. Even our life is long, but we just see the day just once or twice . . ."

"And the Old One?" asked the very small ones, once again.

"He has survived all of his kind . . . He is ancient . . . ancient . . . He has seen more in this world than we can imagine."

Bambi continued on. *"Mosquito songs,"* he thought, *"Mosquito songs . . ."*

He heard a distant, tender, terrified calling.

He listened, went closer, very quietly, always walking through the thickest bushes, always silently, as had long been his way.

Again, he heard it calling, more urgently, bitterly. The voice of his own kind.

"Mother . . . Mother . . . !"

Bambi slipped through the bushes, listened to the call.

There were two fawns standing together in their red coats; a brother and sister, alone and afraid.

"Mother . . . Mother . . . !"

Before they even knew what happened, Bambi stood before them.

He looked at them silently.

"Your mother does not have time for you right now," said Bambi in a stern voice.

He looked them both in the eyes. "Can you not be alone?"

The young boy and his sister stayed silent.

Bambi turned to go and disappeared in the next bush before the two could realize where he went. He wandered off. *"I liked the young boy . . ."* he thought. *"Maybe I will see him again one day, when he is bigger . . ."* He walked further. *"The young girl,"* he thought, *"she was also nice . . . she looked like Faline, when she was still a child."*

He continued on and disappeared into the forest.